PRAISE FOR
DARK SONG

"Giles is a gifted writer of suspense. Her imagery sparkles, her character development is flawless, and this page-turner positively crackles with excitement. . . . Suspense lovers will savor this fast-paced psychological thriller." —*VOYA*, starred review

"Once you cross the line between light and dark, can you ever go back? Gail Giles' chilling novel, *Dark Song*, may be as terrifying to parents as it is to young adult readers. Both will sleep with their lights on! I know I did." —Lois Duncan, author of *Don't Look Behind You* and *Killing Mr. Griffin*

"The queen of YA thrillers does it again with another gripping page-turner in which love and danger meet." —*Kirkus Reviews*

"*Dark Song* is a moving, haunting and unforgettable novel. . . . A powerful study in adolescent rage and its potential to manifest in catastrophic ways." —Terry Trueman, author of *Stuck in Neutral*, a Printz Honor book

"*Dark Song* is an example of Gail Giles doing what Gail Giles does best—exploring the unpretty and making it understandable. Even better, making it relatable." —Jennifer Brown, author of *Hate List*

"Every page brings you closer to the edge of your seat—afraid to keep reading, but unable to stop." —Jo Knowles, author of *Lessons from a Dead Girl*

"This fast-paced psychological thriller will leave readers disturbed, enthralled, and clamoring for more. Fans of the author's *What Happened to Cass McBride?* will thoroughly enjoy this chilling account of a good girl gone bad." —*School Library Journal*

"Readers sucked in by the emotional allure may relish teetering on the edge with Ames." —*Bulletin of the Center for Children's Books*

"Ames and the rest of the Ford family's fall from grace makes for breathless, chilling reading." —*Publishers Weekly*

"Giles' compelling and honest exploration of betrayal and innocence is a real page-turner. Gritty, riveting and impossible to put down." —Courtney Summers, author of *Cracked Up to Be* and *Some Girls Are*

"*Dark Song* is a twisted, chilling descent into the unthinkable. It's also frighteningly believable. A powerful, nerve-wracking read from start to finish. Loved it!" —Laura Wiess, author of *How It Ends*, *Leftovers*, and *Such a Pretty Girl*

"This timely, riveting novel will resonate with readers." —*Booklist*

DARK SONG

by Gail Giles

LITTLE, BROWN AND COMPANY
New York   Boston

Little, Brown and Company
Hachette Book Group
237 Park Avenue, New York, NY 10017
Visit our website at www.lb-teens.com

Little, Brown and Company is a division of Hachette Book Group, Inc.
The Little, Brown name and logo are trademarks of Hachette Book Group, Inc.

The publisher is not responsible for websites (or their content)
that are not owned by the publisher.

First Paperback Edition: October 2011
First published in hardcover in September 2010 by Little, Brown and Company

The characters and events portrayed in this book are fictitious.
Any similarity to real persons, living or dead, is coincidental
and not intended by the author.

Library of Congress Cataloging-in-Publication Data
Giles, Gail.
Dark song / by Gail Giles.
p. cm.
Summary: After her father loses his job and she finds out that her parents have lied to her, fifteen-year-old Ames feels betrayed enough to become involved with a criminal who will stop at nothing to get what he wants.
ISBN 978-0-316-06886-4 (hc) / ISBN 978-0-316-06887-1 (pb)
[1. Family problems—Fiction 2. Secrets—Fiction. 3. Criminals—Fiction.]
I. Title.
PZ7.G3923Dar 2010
[Fic]—dc22   2010006888

10 9 8 7 6 5 4 3 2 1

RRD-C

This book was set in Sabon; the display face is Monotype Modern.
Book design by Ben Mautner

Printed in the United States of America

Always and always and always for Jim Giles and Josh Jakubik, my heroes
—G. G.

Dark has a sound. A song.

Marc said he heard it when he creeped houses.
The song the predator's heart sings when it
hears the heart of the prey.

I heard it now.

Marc said it had always been in me.
Lurking. Waiting for me to hear.

The breathing from my parents' room was slow and steady.
This was the time of reckoning.
I punched the number into the cell phone and dialed.
Marc answered.
"You ready for this?"
I didn't respond.
"It will be just us when it's done.
No one will ever hurt you again," he said.

"The kitchen door is open," I said.
"Let's get it done."

Part

1

Part 1

BEFORE

Christmas was near, and Boulder looked like a fairy tale. Seriously. Tons of snow, twinkly lights strung through the aspen downtown and along all the rooflines. Somehow you'd expect Cinderella rather than Santa because it had such a delicate touch.

Our house was a fairy tale, too. Ten-foot tree in our living room that soared two stories. The miniature white lights laced the thick branches like bits of snow caught by the sun and every ornament was a work of art, placed just so. My mom wouldn't have it any other way. The shiny top of the grand piano reflected the lights and put out a glow, and the array of expensively wrapped presents was a show all of its own. The walls gleamed the color of rich butter whipped with cream and the chandelier was covered with a silk shade. Something Mom's interior designer insisted was a "must."

I gave Mom a hard time about her obsession with decorating the house, but I had to admit, it was warm and "charming" and felt like home base. What Mom lacked in warmth, she tried to make up for with our snug nest and by doing Mom-type things with us—folding table napkins into swans, creating flower arrangements, that kind of thing.

Today Mom was teaching us to make ratatouille. Chrissy had sorted the veggies and was teaching her bear to color while Mom and I chopped and diced, making sure the vegetable pieces were all the same size, when Dad plowed into the kitchen and spread both arms wide.

"Stop what you're doing and go pack. Heavy, heavy winter wear and bathing suits. No further clues provided," Dad said. He arched one eyebrow and wiggled it. "Our plane leaves at midnight." He swept Mom and me to the side, pushed all the chopped veggies into a plastic container. "I'm totally serious. We'll be back in three days; you can finish this"—he eyed the chopped eggplant as he snapped on the lid—"when we get back." He snuggled his chin into the curve of Mom's neck.

When he pulled back, he surveyed our stunned faces. "Nobody's moving! Go, go, go! One carry-on bag. Jeans, boots, sweaters, long underwear, flannel PJs. Wear the heavy coat, pack the bathing suit."

He clapped his hands. "Shoo!"

We shooed.

After flying for umpteen hours we landed in Seattle, then Anchorage, Alaska, then Fairbanks, then to a toy plane and a runway made of packed snow in Circle, Alaska. Some man rented us what I think was his own 4Runner and we drove to a hotel and a string of cabins in the middle of THE BIG WHITE NOWHERE. Circle Hot Springs. It was daytime by the clock but dark to the eyeballs. Off to the right of the hotel was a spooky-looking glow and lots of fog.

"This is your Christmas present," Dad said. "It's minus thirty and we swim in the hot springs and everything is right for the aurora borealis. Can you imagine?"

We clapped. We didn't have to imagine. Dad did that for us. He was our moon and stars and I guess Mom was our gravity, but right now, she was floating a little, too.

We checked into a cabin. "The hotel is upscale, but it's booked because of the aurora." Dad glanced at Mom. "Be prepared. The cabins are described as 'rustic.'"

Mom put her hand to her forehead. "Randal."

"I know," Dad said. "That translates as 'primitive.'"

"Roach motel." Mom was a hotel snob.

"The hotel restaurant is first class." He swung open the door, and if the cold weren't frosting our butts, we wouldn't have set a toe in the place. Stains on the carpets, sagging mattresses, mismatched furniture that was past due for the Dumpster—or possibly came from the Dumpster. It made summer camp look like Oz.

"In, in, everybody, so I can turn up the heat."

When Dad closed the door I noted the corker. The thing that turned this room from a disaster into a cartoon.

Nailed over the top of the door with roofing nails was a flap of shaggy carpet. To keep out the draft.

Mom looked at it. Her eyes got big. Then she started laughing. Full and deep. I don't think I'd ever heard that sound from her. It was so infectious that soon we were all laughing with her.

"Randal," she said. "This, *this*, is the perfect vacation." Mom tried to catch her breath. "I always worry, what will go wrong, what *can* go wrong. At first I thought this is as bad as the places I lived with my mother. It's... well, look around, this place is totally"—she searched for the words—"disaster-proofed. Like what Garp called his house. The disaster has been and gone."

She was right. But the sheets were clean. The duvets were soft and thick. There was only about two hours of light and those were sunrise followed by sunset, both spectacular in the extreme. The stars were molten intensity in the black sky and felt close enough to grab.

The hot springs were another form of magic, covered with a misty fog from the natural heat hitting the cold air. In the frigid weather my bathing suit had to be buried under my parka and jeans, but I managed to hit the water in record time.

Soon the rest of the Fords were bobbing next to me. Chrissy with her floaties. The heavenly, spa-hot water was misty gray like the fog around us. We were surrounded above and below. Floating in a warm cocoon of the now. No future in sight.

"Everybody under," Dad shouted.

We all ducked under the water, then bobbed back up and within seconds our hair frosted, lighting us with a halo effect.

"We look like those monkeys!" Chrissy shrieked. She'd seen a poster of Japanese monkeys in a mountain hot spring, their ruffs tipped with ice. Dad made monkey hoots and splashed Chrissy, but I pushed away.

"Stop," I urged. "Stop and look up."

And there it was. Green and red and white undulating across the skies. The stars blinking in and out as the colors dipped and then rose and swirled. We pulled together, floating in our cocoon of mist and warmth, watching color as we'd never seen it. Pure, flowing, rippling. It was a thing of wonder. It lasted about twenty minutes and we didn't say a single word.

As the colors faded and drifted away, Chrissy waved a good-bye. "It's a nighttime rainbow. So it's good luck, right?"

"Maybe so, Chrissy," Dad said. "I hope so."

"I want to remember this forever," I said.

But memories don't always reveal the whole picture.

And some memories lie.

NO SIGNS?

We spent Christmas Day kind of low-key, opening the presents. Mom: diamond bracelet, understated but gorgeous, a small painting by an up-and-coming artist who was all the rage. Dad: yet another watch, an automatic watch winder for six watches, new hiking boots, new cross-country skis, tennis racquet. Chrissy: bears, books, puzzles, a little electric car, hiking boots, half a ton of clothes, a set of watercolors in a cherrywood box and an easel that even I envied, toys on top of more toys. Me: sweaters, jeans, books, a new laptop, more clothes, and new hiking boots.

One of my gifts is my annual post-Christmas, pre–New Year's slumber party. Since we practice the fine art of table decoration and place setting and have enough china and crystal to seat, well, *China*, it's strange that Mom almost never has people to the house. Too chaotic, maybe. So it's a big honking deal for me to have a party. It's always the twenty-eighth. Everyone comes at noon and stays until noon the next day. Mom and Carmen, the housekeeper, make a huge brunch and we have fake mimosas in champagne flutes.

We had eaten lunch and were camped out in my room rehashing who got what, who was doing what, who was doing whom. I was never doing whom. I had one date so far on my résumé. With a total nerd to a school party. Misery with music.

Emily Keifer, my best friend, was painting her toenails dark purple. "So let me get this straight. You went to Nowheresville In The Snow? And you loved, loved, *loved* it? Days in boots and hats with flaps and nothing to see but igloos and penguins? Like we don't have enough snow here?"

"How could you tell if a guy was ripped or not under all those clothes?" asked Layla Emerson, whose father had to pay big premiums to get his helium-head daughter into our prestigious school.

Em pointed the polish wand at me. "I would never want a family isolation vacation. Nobody wants that."

Reggie Wilcox, who was sprawled near Em, waved a French-tipped nail. "Cooped up in the boonies with your little sister and parents, with no television or Internet. In, like, a creepy hotel? No way."

I looked at anorexic Kim Banks, who was deciding if she would eat half an M&M or a whole peanut. She rolled her eyes. "Girl, you're my friend and everything, but that's kind of...*mental*."

They were right. None of them spent all that much time with their families. Not to mention the other differences. I wasn't painting my nails. Or cruising the fashion mags. I was kind of the cuckoo's egg in the sparrow's nest. I needed to shift their focus away from me and onto themselves.

"All of you have estrogen poisoning," I said.

"Oh. My. God," Kim announced, "Ames is a '*mo*!"

I threw a pillow at her. Em flattened out on the floor in mock surrender. "Why does everyone go there first?" she grumbled. "Ames is *not* a 'mo. She's just not a girlie girl and so only nerds like her and she thinks nerds are repulso."

"Who doesn't?" Layla asked.

"Girl nerds," I said.

"Aren't all girl nerds 'mos?" Layla seemed serious.

Em turned to her. "Layla, look at me and try to concentrate. If there weren't any hetero female nerds to hook up with the male nerds, how would we ever get baby nerds?"

Layla finally got that we were messing with her. "I still think staying in, like, an igloo with your parents for vacation is lame. It's as close to being a nerd as it gets."

"Movie time," I said.

As we headed for the home theater room, we passed my dad.

"Hey, ladies, what's up? Is this Slumber Party time?"

"Too true, Mr. Ford. Weird seeing you home in the middle of the day," Em commented. "If I ever saw my stepdad home in daylight, my vampire theory would go right out the window."

He smiled. "Early New Year's resolution. Take more time for my family. It's something I want to do for Mrs. Ford. Spend time at home. Nobody dies wishing they had worked a few more days, right?"

"Earl might," Em said, referring to her stepdad again. She'd never admit it, but she practically worshipped the guy. "We haven't seen much of him since Christmas Day."

My smooth, unflappable Dad seemed to, I don't know, "hitch" a little. Like a pained hiccup, or a misfired synapse. Then he was flashing his teeth again. "Why don't I make you a big batch of popcorn?"

"None for me, sir. But thanks," Kim said.

"I'll have her share," I said. "Thanks, Dad."

We went to the movie room and argued over chick flick or gore fest. We settled on creepy house story that ended in gore fest. It fit my strange and unidentifiable feeling of unease.

Kim, Layla, Reggie, and, occasionally, Em squealed and hid their eyes when various characters were beheaded, eviscerated, impaled, or otherwise bloodily dispatched during the movie. I watched almost without blinking, eating popcorn more rapidly with each death.

"That was so gross," Layla said.

"You loved it," I told her.

"I *didn't*," Reggie insisted. "Those poor cheerleaders were so sweet. And that crazy girl who killed them...she was ugly."

"She was ugly because they ran her off the road and her car caught on fire. She was scarred for life."

"Ames, that was an accident. They only meant to scare her," Kim reminded me. "She stole that blond girl's boyfriend, after all."

"Em, straighten them out!" I jabbed her with my elbow. "The cheerleaders ruined that girl's life. They got what they had coming."

Everyone stared. I didn't realize I had been shouting.

Em finally broke the silence. "I had no idea little ole Ames is a repressed serial killer. Sleep with one eye open, girlfriends."

"Pfft," Reggie whiffed. "Ames would ask her parents for permission before she killed anyone."

"Chick flick?" Em suggested.

Three hands waved.

"Sexbots," I sniffed.

The Christmas break flew by and Dad didn't go into work. He didn't take clients to dinner. He did huddle up with the phone a lot with his study doors closed. But he watched Chrissy's penguin movies and her mermaid movies and played Old Maid and Uno a bazillion times and we smacked each other around with Wii boxing and tennis. He let me win at boxing but never at tennis.

Em called just once. "What's happening at *su casa*? Anything out of the ordinary?"

"We went hiking to break in our new boots. We played Monopoly and Scrabble," I said.

"Hiking. I get a visual of flannel and down vests and

heinous footwear. I shudder and my skin crawls. Don't. Speak. Of. It. Again."

"We made Julia Child's beef stew. Chrissy made pudding. All ordinary. What's up?"

"There's buzzy on the buzz front. I was at a party, the one you didn't go to, and there was a whisper campaign that shut down when I came around. But I caught your dad's name."

"Dad?"

"Too true. Has he been acting weird?"

"Nope. He's been home the whole break. He's on the phone a lot so I think he's checking in at work. You know my dad—if anything was up, I'd know about it."

"You know that's a crock, right?" Em said.

"I don't want to argue. The buzz must be about one of your many dads."

"Step. Stepdads. You have a point. So, you're good?"

"We're good. The whole family is good," I said.

Mom had a tree-down-before-New-Year's fetish so we spent a day storing all the lights and ornaments and other decorations into labeled boxes under her supervision. Dad would tease Mom by purposefully putting an item in the wrong box just to get her motor revving. He called her the Commander because all the orders in the house were hers. That was okay. If Mom weren't a little overcontrolling sometimes—okay, all of the time—our family would've been gag-worthy perfect.

THE BUZZ

When school started again, I piled into the backseat of
Em's mom's Escalade. "It's so great to get back to school.
Less rules than at home," I said.

"Ames complaining about Mumsy? That must mean
the Commandant gave you a long New Year's list of rules
or chores or whatevers," Em said.

"We call her the Commander, and no, she didn't. She's
not mean, Em, she's just really, really"—Em and I drew it
out singsong-like together—"r-e-a-l-l-y organized." Em
and I don't giggle but we sort of snort, so we snorted.

"You two are disrespectful," Em's mom said. "I shudder to think what you say about me."

Em's response was immediate. "We say that you are beautiful and wonderful in the extreme, and you are *so* sweet that you're going to give me a credit card with no limit this afternoon. And I'll swoon with the awesomeness of my mother goddess."

Em didn't wait for her mother to bat an eyelash and continued in almost the same breath. "Your mom seriously needs to loosen up. Have I mentioned that before?"

"A few too many times," I said. "She does sometimes. We oil up her joints on occasion and it lasts awhile."

To be honest, I needed my joints to be oiled up on occasion, too. That's why Em and I were such great friends. There was something in me that wanted loose. I didn't know what it was. Em usually drank and toked without me as her accomplice. One of us had to be straight to find the way home when she was under the influence. Without me, she would've shown up buck naked on YouTube a year ago.

Em hopped to some gossip and we rode on to school. We bailed out of the car, and soon as we were out of earshot, Em started plotting. "By the way, Mom's been way too interested in your Picnic with the Penguins vacation. She's been quizzing me like a game-show contestant. Let's cut first hour and hit a coffee shop. We've got more important things to discuss."

"Seriously? You think I'm going to cut class? We can talk at lunch."

"Arrrgggh. This is, like, *major*."

"Drama Queen."

"Geek, Nerd. Dud."

"See you at lunch then," I said. "And penguins are on the other side of the world, Your Dimness."

"I could care," Em retorted, and we parted where the corridors merged.

I headed toward my first class wondering what Em was stressing about this time.

I bumped shoulders with Edwin Myer as I entered the door to our calculus class. He's the nerd of my famous only date. Having inherited no DNA for tact from my mother, I had refused a second date by telling him that I found him boring. Okay, a little harsh, but if I have to pick between Edwin feeling the sting of rejection and me feeling the horror of death by dreariness, I'm not apologizing.

Now, Edwin wants to prove he's "dangerous." He does this by baiting our teacher Mr. Bivens.

"Hey, Ames. I've got a good one today." He winked at me.

I guess he thought it was a bad-boy wink. He looked like a nerd with a twitch. We took our seats and in no time Edwin was casting his lure.

"Mr. Bivens, we're studying etymology in our English class and I know this is calculus not algebra, but the root word *alg* translates to pain. Don't you think that's interesting?"

Quiet snickering.

Mr. Bivens, who clearly thought Edwin was a dolt but was more polite than Edwin, sighed. "Algebra is not taken from the Latin but from Arabic. Its name is derived from the Islamic Persian mathematician, Muhammad ibn Mūsā al-Khwārizmī who is considered the father of algebra. The word *Al-Jabr* means 'reunion.'"

Edwin's blush showed he clearly didn't appreciate being one-upped in the trivia department. "Maybe. *Alg* means pain. I just don't think it's a coincidence."

Edwin got his laughs. Mr. Bivens allowed them with a courtly bow.

Edwin was trumped with old-world graciousness.

Lesson missed.

Dorks like Edwin don't understand that you don't impress anyone, you aren't the big shot, if you go after your opponent by tweaking him or biting him on the toe.

Get savage and go for the jugular or shut up. Go for it or go down.

At lunchtime I strode into the cafeteria and headed for the table, where Kim studied a stalk of celery and Layla and Reggie leaned heads close, whispering. Em cut me off and herded me off to an empty table in the corner. "Here, I got your lunch. We don't need to talk to them."

"Why not?"

"First, Reggie is telling everyone that your slumber party is straight out of fifth grade. Parents, no alcohol, no dope, no porn, no guys. Popcorn and movies, fake mimosas. Layla thinks all the time you spend with your parents is creepy and Kim thinks the fact that your parents never have adults to the house is Witness Protection Program strange."

"These are my friends?"

"Oh, please," Em said. "We say worse about them. Now, they're whispering about other stuff, too."

"Oh, don't tell me they're that stupid. They *do* think we're lesbians?" I was being sarcastic, but the fifth grade comments made me want to kick in a few laser-whitened teeth.

"Sorry, being gay would make you more interesting," Em joked. Then she leaned in and the always-a-smart-remark mask Em wore was gone. "Nope, there's something in the air. I told you, the Boulder Beehive is buzzing. My mom has been way too friendly over the holidays, pumping me for info about you and your family. 'Ames left town so unexpectedly. Then her dad took such a long time off work. Isn't that really unusual for him? How does Ames seem? Her mom? Did you see her dad? How was he?'"

I put down the Coke I was sipping. "Why—"

Em put up a finger to stop me from talking. "None of this was all at once and none of it's direct quotes, but when was the last time my mom was so interested in my friends? I mean she's all with the good manners to everyone when she sees them, but once they're out of sight, trust me, out of mind."

"Em!" I put both palms on the table top. "Will you get to the point?"

Em looked around and lowered her voice. "There's something going on. It's about your dad and his job. But I don't know what it is. I know if I ask Mom she won't tell me. I thought your dad or mom would have told you something if the whisper campaign is already this heavy. The info from Reggie or the Dumbo Duo isn't to be trusted."

"What info? Em, spit it out."

"I just said." Em appeared to be losing patience with me. "Something about your dad and his job. If people are whispering, it's not a promotion. There's something wrong." Her face and tone were filled with concern.

23

I sat a minute. Then—the first flicker of mistrust.

Dad had been tense. And he'd been on the phone in a closed room. A lot. I shut my eyes. Pushed it away. Away. Gone. I took a swig of my drink and breathed easy again. This was nothing Dad couldn't explain.

"Nope. If there's something big going on, there's one thing I know for sure. Dad doesn't know about it, or the whisper campaign is wrong. No secrets in our house."

By the time school was out I can honestly say I'd brushed off any uneasiness Em had managed to dangle before me at lunch. I danced my way through the back door, hooked my backpack on the brass hook that waited for it like a quiet butler, and stopped short to see Dad sitting at the kitchen table.

"Hey, big guy," I said. "What are you doing home?" I kissed his cheek. His breath already smelled of his Happy-to-Be-Home-Jack-Attack. That's the one glass of Jack Daniel's Dad has when he gets home and loosens his tie and props up his feet. It's a ritual.

He smiled. Wide smile. Happy, happy. "Playing a little

hooky. Took off at noon. You won't tell?" My dad is the giant clock that keeps my world ticking at just the right speed. He's tall, lean, and athletic. Makes you feel like he could single-handedly take on a mountain lion to protect you.

"Can I play hooky tomorrow?"

"Nope, you have a test tomorrow."

That's my family. We're kind of in each other's pockets. Know what everybody's doing all the time. So it felt off to see him home when he hadn't said anything this morning.

"Where's the Commander?" I asked. Mom is always at the computer desk in the kitchen when I come home. She and Chrissy play educational computer games together or Mom plans menus and Chrissy draws and colors. Lately Mom has been teaching Chrissy the wonders of origami.

"Mom's upstairs. She has a little headache. I told her I'd grill some fish for dinner. Six, okay?"

I shrugged. It had been a full thirty minutes since I'd talked to my friends and I had some IMing to do.

When I buzzed past Mom's door I saw that she had her eyes covered with a wet washcloth. This wasn't a bit of a headache. Wet washcloth meant migraine. That meant major stress.

I swung into my little sister's room. I can always count on Chrissy to have the inside story. "What's up, Munchkin?"

"Nothing," Chrissy murmured. She was teaching school to her row of dolls and stuffed bears. "Dad's home. He and Mom whispered for a long time. Then Mom got a bad headache," Chrissy said. She's six, but she's a great reporter. Just the facts and she tends to get them right.

"Do you know what they whispered about?" Whisper had a whole new sense of worry for me now.

"Nope."

"Why not?" I asked.

"Sent me to my room. Told me to close my door."

Close the door? Again, worrisome, but…everything was fine. "Later," I said.

"Mr. Brown Bear has been bad. I have to make him

stay after school. What is that called? The big word they use in your school?"

"Detention."

"Mr. Brown." Chrissy frowned at one of the stuffed animals. "I detention you."

I left her uncorrected. I liked it. It had clout.

IT'LL ALL BE FINE

Mom picked at her grilled fish. Her eyes were puffy and red. She said her allergies were kicking up. Dad had made chocolate pudding for dessert. Dinner was quiet and he had three glasses of wine instead of his usual two.

"The pinot noir is perfect with the fish," Dad said. "Sure you won't have a glass?"

"You're having enough for both of us." Mom smiled, but her face was tight.

Something was...I couldn't put my finger on it. It was

like when a picture was hanging just out of square but I couldn't decide which way it needed adjusting. We usually discussed happy stuff at dinner. Schedules. Trips. Problems went away by themselves if you didn't talk about them. Dad made bad vibes vanish with chatter and fun. Mom cold-shouldered it and starved it to death. Dad tried for some chat tonight but this time it was like those dubbed movies when the words and the mouths aren't moving in sync. It made me fidgety.

Our big kitchen felt claustrophobic, and the quiet was way too loud. I felt...yeah, unbalanced. Maybe the whisper campaign, the buzz, had merit.

Dad finished his pudding. Put his spoon across the edge of his plate. "Girls, there's something we need to discuss as a family. You don't need to worry about this. Not even a little. It won't affect your lives at all. But your mother and I want you to know everything."

I put my spoon down. Dad was all wrong with the Robo-speak. Short, choppy sentences. Not his easy-breezy tale-telling style. He seemed...rehearsed?

Something shadowy entered my head. Em rehearsed

when she lied to her parents. No one has to rehearse the truth, right?

"I've been let go from my job. It's all very complicated. They're downsizing. Several people have been let go." Dad sighed. He toyed with his pudding spoon.

I sat in my chair feeling like someone was tugging on the rug underneath. *Downsized*. That sounded a lot like "fired" wearing a prom dress.

"We get a severance package, which is quite a bit of money, and benefits, so that's why your lives won't be different. Nothing will change except that my job now will be looking for a job. I'll be at home for a while doing a job search." He dropped his spoon. Pushed his bowl back and laced his fingers, hands on the antique oak table. "It could take a few months. Upper-level jobs like mine take a while to find. It goes without saying that I'd rather not move."

The muscles in Mom's jaw were hard under her skin. Dad looked up and smiled. The smile he uses for corporate photos, the one with his teeth set together and his mouth just so.

He looked at me, then at Chrissy, but avoided Mom. "It's important to me that my girls' lives aren't disrupted. Nobody loses their friends or routines. I'll be looking for things where I can commute from Boulder." Dad's smile seemed to gain more confidence. "Everything will be fine."

But Dad smelled of guilt. He was *too* cheerful, too... toothy, then backing away too fast like a pup that doesn't want you to find the wet spot on the carpet.

Mom folded her linen napkin, creasing the edges with her thumb in short, hard strokes. "I can't stay here right now. I still have a..." She shot a venomous glare at Dad. "Headache. I hope you can manage without me." She left.

I wanted to hug Dad, tell him that money didn't mean anything as long as he was here with us. But Mom had somehow put a frost on all of us.

Before I even had a chance to do anything, Dad stood up and did that lame thing like he was pinching off Chrissy's nose and said, "Remember, my new job now is finding a job. I'll be at the computer."

And then he left, too.

This had happened before—never. Nobody left the table without permission from the rest of us. We had rituals. Mom did the dishes and I helped. She asked about my day, and I chatted about the homework I had. I told edited versions of what Em was up to. Sometimes Dad and Chrissy stayed in the kitchen and we all told jokes or made plans for the weekend.

Now Dad had just dropped a major bomb and both of them left, no discussion, no questions about how Chrissy and I might be feeling about it. It was like someone made a marionette Dad and dangled him into place, eyes painted on and jaw moving but the words coming from some other direction.

Em always told me that there should be a big neon sign on adults' heads that says RARELY TRUSTWORTHY.

I had always believed what Dad said. And Dad was saying it was no big deal.

End of story.

I gave Dad some time and space while I did my homework, then went down to his office. He had a glass of Jack

Daniel's on his desk and he changed screens when he heard me come in. Writing cover letters when you're a grown man must be embarrassing.

"Ames, shouldn't you be doing homework? I'm kind of busy here," Dad said.

When had he not rolled his chair back and welcomed me in for a visit? What's the word for that? Rebuffed.

"Dad, can we drop the act? I know this has to be a lousy day for you. But it's just a day. You're my dad. And you're acting like I'm not going to love you or something because you don't have a job."

Dad rubbed his forehead with his fingertips and wouldn't meet my eyes.

"Hey, you're, like, WonderDad or something. You taught me to ride a bike and swim and ski. You chased all the monsters out of the closet and from under the bed. Anybody who can do that can get another job. It'll be a piece of cake." Dad still stared at the jumbled surface of his desk. I drifted over and slid my arm across his shoulders. "I've got your back, Dad. I know Mom is freaking out, but she can't help it."

Dad made a throat-clearing sound and reached for his glass.

"She'll calm down," I said.

Dad took a long swallow, draining his glass. "Maybe not this time," he said. When he looked up at me, his eyes were wet. He rolled his chair so that my arm fell away from his shoulders.

NOT SO FINE

Mom's eyes had luggage underneath them the next morning, and she peered at us through reddened slits. Had she cried all night?

"Allergies," she said. But there was no sniffling or sneezing.

"Mom, if you're crying because Dad lost his job, just say so."

Mom's back stiffened. I mean, I could see her seize up like a board. Her eyes flashed at me through the puffed slits. "You'll not say a word to anyone about this, Ames. I have allergies."

Her voice was quiet, but her meaning roared: *You know nothing. Stay out of this.*

"Are you *kidding* me?" I took my last bite of breakfast, Cheerios with chocolate milk, my elementary school hold-over that Em declared gross beyond all reasonable thought. "How do you think I'm supposed to keep the fact that my dad's *unemployed* a secret from the rest of the world? That's *insane.*"

"Ames, don't be such a drama queen. All I'm saying is just don't repeat our family's business to your school friends."

I turned and stomped to the front door so she could hear my anger loud and clear. It wasn't unusual for Mom and me to be like two rocks inside a tin can. We'd bounce and bang into each other, ricocheting off walls, me hoping with each chip we took out of each other that our edges would wear smooth and we could find a place to fit together.

That obviously wasn't going to happen today.

*   *   *

Dad drove us toward school and stopped at Em's. She bounced into the car and did a double take when she saw who was behind the wheel. "Hey, Mr. Ford."

"Hi, Emily. Mrs. Ford is under the weather today."

Under the weather? Dad lied to Em in front of me. That meant I would have to lie to my best friend to support Dad's lie, or else make him look like a reptile.

Why doesn't he want anyone to know he's been "downsized"? My stomach went on the spin cycle. Suddenly I couldn't think of a thing to say. We could have been traveling to a funeral. Em gave me her through-the-eyelashes look, which meant I'd be grilled later.

When we got out at school, Em didn't even wait for the car to get out of sight. "Did he catch you having sex? Robbing an ATM? Uploading a nudie picture of yourself on Facebook? How long is he gonna be your guard dog?" She was walking backward in front of me.

Then, a sure sign my life had already changed: I would lie to my best friend for the first time. "Dad just wants to hook out from work today. Says he's stressed out. He calls it a mental health day."

"I'm so not buying what you're selling." Em dropped back to walking beside me. "What's such a big secret?"

I'd given Dad a pass this time with all the stress, but the irritation clung to me like a bad aftertaste. By the time we reached the T in the school corridor, I was still not telling.

Em turned her back on me and walked away. "Do not talk to me again until you're ready to tell the truth." She flung this over her shoulder.

Tears stung my eyes. Kim Banks stopped dead center in front of me. "Is the world coming to an end? Is Ames Ford crying? What's the deal?"

I ground the heel of my hand into my eyes. "Allergies," I said.

The school day was a disaster. The eyes of my friends, my not-friends, and my enemies seemed to either bore into me or avoid me with purpose all day. What did they know? Was Em mad enough to be gossiping? Nobody I knew well worked at Dad's company, but what about someone else's dad or mom or uncle? One of those people I never paid attention to? Freshmen? Losers? The NMKs (Not My Kind)?

I couldn't make sense of my best subject. My calculus test could have been hieroglyphics for all I could make of it. I scribbled on it a little, stared at it a lot, and mostly sat with my forehead resting against my hand. Even Edwin acted like I was radioactive.

Math had always made sense. Nothing subjective there. Apply the rules and get the right answer. Not now. If I couldn't read the problem, how could I hope to find an answer?

I sealed off. Walked down the halls without making eye contact. Didn't speak to anyone. I skipped lunch because I didn't know what to say to Em. I sat outside on the steps and pretended to read.

Em's mom picked us up that day. For the first time I can remember, Emily sat in the passenger seat and I was alone in the back. Em's mom appeared a bit surprised, but I guess she figured she'd get the 411 when she and Em were alone.

Then she said something totally strange. "Ames, how are your mom and dad holding up?"

"They're fine..." I said, startled for a second. Then I found myself saying for the third time that day, "Mom just isn't feeling well today and Dad's playing hooky. Mental health day, y'know."

Em snorted. I shot her a death-ray glare that should have caused blood to leak out of her ears and eyes.

Em's mom nodded, but her eyes in the rearview mirror as she searched my face held...pity?

What did she know? I felt like everybody was invited to the party but me. I chewed the inside of my cheek as Em yakked nonstop with her mom.

As soon as I got home I slammed through the front door and headed straight upstairs.

"Dad made cookies," Chrissy yelled from the kitchen.

I stopped. Turned and came back down the stairs.

Dad and Chrissy were chowing down on chocolate chip cookies and milk. The counters and sink were cluttered with the signs of baking. One of Chrissy's bears was seated on a couple of phone books and had a plate with cookies in front of him. The Beatrix Potter tea set that Mom had brought Chrissy from England was laid on a lace tablecloth and the good silver spoons were at Mr. Brown's service.

"We're having a tea party, only with milk," Chrissy announced with a grin.

"I'll get you a plate," Dad offered.

WonderDad was back. Amusing Chrissy. Making her feel safe and loved. Inviting me to the party. I sighed in relief.

"Sure." I pulled out a chair while Chrissy handed me a ludicrously tiny teacup and saucer. Dad poured a dribble of milk and the cookie overhung the plate by inches.

"Chocolate chip, my fave."

We munched and sipped.

"I don't know about you, but I think Chrissy, Mr. Brown, and I make a mean chocolate chip cookie," Dad said.

"I agree," I said. "But I hope Mr. Brown washed his hands if he handled the dough."

"He didn't do anything but read the recipe off the bag of chips," Chrissy said.

"Since when can he read?" I asked.

"Dad taught him today."

I put up my hand to high-five Dad. "Way to go, Big Man—"

"I thought you were supposed to be getting a new job." We looked up to see Mom standing in the kitchen doorway.

"What did you say?" Dad's tone was stunned.

Mom's angry burst of words popped like bubble wrap. "First it was you had to get supplies from the office store, then it was you would amuse Chrissy until Ames got home, and now all of you are here wasting time."

Dad stared for a moment. "I'm having a good time with my children. How is that wasting time?"

Mom glared at Dad but spoke to Chrissy and me. "Go upstairs now and close your doors."

I didn't want to leave Dad. He looked wounded, his shoulders drooping as he shook his head at me. "Your mother and I need to talk."

I turned to him and opened my mouth. Dad shook his head again. "Let's not make this worse." He nodded toward Chrissy. "Ames. Go ahead and take Chrissy upstairs and don't say anything."

I took Chrissy to her room. "Why is Mommy so mad?" she asked, on the verge of crying.

"I think she just needs to vent."

"I don't know that word."

"She just needs to get mad at somebody, anybody, because she's upset. Then she'll calm down and be fine."

"How does that help? Doesn't it just hurt people's feelings?"

Chrissy was six and smarter than all of us put together. Were we all born smart and then learned to be stupid? Do we lose our honesty when we lose our innocence?

ANGER IS EASY

I put the PRIVACY PLEASE sign on my bedroom doorknob. It was a present Mom and Dad had given me on my thirteenth birthday. A super-size symbol of mutual trust. Not to be overused. Only when the need to be alone and getting my thoughts in order was crucial.

Before I could catch hold of a single thought, notion, or idea, my cell rang.

"Why didn't you tell me?" Em demanded. "Do you know how totally embarrassing it was for my mother to know every last detail and there I was, clueless? If I didn't

feel, like, so sorry for you, I'd never speak to you again."
Em talked so fast her words were like handfuls of rocks
thrown against my window, clattering too fast and too
loud to make sense.

Embarrassing for *her*?

I hung up.

It rang again. God, I hated speed dial.

"Okay," Em said. "I'm talking too fast. This is, like,
huge and I'm hyper and so shocked. So, where do we start?
Tell me everything. Are you going to be poor now? Will
you have to wear ugly clothes?"

That did it. I fell onto the bed and laughed. Seriously lost it. Stomach-hurting, eye-leaking, nose-snorting
laughter.

"Em, we already wear pleated plaid skirts, flannel
blazers with a godawful crest, and a white shirt that has a
Peter Pan collar...and brown shoes? We look like refu-
gees from a World War II movie. I'd love to be poor enough
to wear public school clothes."

"Don't squab with me. I mean our civilian clothes. But
anyway, what gives? How come your dad got fired?"

"He was downsized."

"When was he upsized?"

I snorted again. "Good one. Em, I don't know what's going on." I sighed. "Dad says his company let a bunch of people go, that he got a big wad of money and nothing will change, that it will just take a while for him to get a new job and blah, blah. But they don't want anybody to know about it. Mom's been crying since yesterday and…" I stopped again. "Dad's acting strange."

"Strange how?"

"That's the problem. I can't grab hold of it. The only thing I can say for sure is that he didn't hug us last night."

"Definitely criminal behavior. I'm calling 911 this minute. Arrest the man."

"Em, I'm serious. I feel like I'm being lied to…"

"I *am* sorry, Tweety Bird, but welcome to the club. I've been trying to get this through your head since we were, like, ten. Parents lie. It's what they do. And it's why it's only fair that we lie back to them." Em sighed. "You've been such a late bloomer."

"I guess. But I hate it. It felt good to believe them."

"They've been lying to you since they told you that Santa brought your Christmas gifts. I haven't trusted them since," Em said.

"Santa Claus was fun."

"He was bogus." The singsonging on "bogus" strung it out.

I remembered how confused I had been when I had seen all the Santas in downtown Denver. How Mom explained them away. "Point for Emily's team."

"Look, Tweety, after your very untrustworthy parents go to sleep, put a magnet against the security alarm contact on your window and bail. Call and I'll pick you up. There's more to your dad's story. I don't know much. But Earl is involved and that can't be good. I'll tell the little I know and we'll have a frisky night. It will be payback for your dear ones ruining your day."

I thought a second. Em's stepdad Earl was a high-priced criminal lawyer. Em was right—if he was involved...it couldn't be good.

"Why the hell not," I said.

Dinner was quiet. Almost. The only one talking was Chrissy.

"Dan got in trouble today in kindergarten," she said. She loves to say "kindergarten" because it's such a long word.

Mom picked at her salad and Dad acted like buttering his roll took all of his brainpower.

"What did he do?" I asked.

"When Ms. Riley handed out the cookies, he grabbed three when he's only supposed to take two."

"That wasn't polite," I said.

"He said he's bigger and needs more," the little reporter said, without judgment.

Mom pushed her salad away and stood up. "Dan should have realized that and saved up a little." She stormed out of the room.

Chrissy looked at the swinging kitchen door. "That wouldn't work. He'd have less cookies each day if he was saving them, right?"

By this time Dad was up and going after Mom.

I looked at Chrissy. "Eat your dinner. This isn't about cookies," I told her. As if I had a hint what it was really about. Now I felt like I was lying to my sister, too.

Great. Just great.

The clattering of silverware seemed deafening even though it was just two forks—mine and Chrissy's—making the racket. After we finished, I started clearing the plates.

I want everything to feel normal again, I thought.

Right that minute I would've given anything to be cleaning plates and chatting with my mother. When we cleaned, it was the closest we came to fitting. It was a wind-down time. I think it was her strange way of hugging. Cleaning was Mom's drug of choice. She gets mellow and happy when she cleans. Probably because she's a clear thinker and cleaning must keep the thought pathways open for business. I liked to be around her then, since we would rarely butt heads.

I kept hoping Mom or Dad would come back downstairs and join me. No such luck. So when I finished the dishes, I headed for Dad's study. The French doors were closed, and I could hear his beyond-bad country music. We used to tease him about it. His back was to the doors so I tapped on the glass pane. He glanced over his shoulder...and waved me away.

Mom and Chrissy were in Chrissy's room, where Chrissy was giving Mom the rest of the kindergarten scoop. I went in.

"Ms. Riley read us a book about wild things. This boy named Max was bad to his mom. She called him a wild thing. Max became the king of the wild things. And they rumpused." Chrissy paused. "I don't know how to rumpus. But it looked like fun."

Mom smiled. "It's a wonderful book, Chrissy. I read it when I was a girl."

"Can you buy it for me?" Chrissy said. "I want to read again about the rumpusing." I loved the way she was so precise when she talked.

Mom got up. "We'll check it out from the library."

"I want to buy it," Chrissy insisted. "I want to put it on my shelf."

Chrissy pointed to her shelves clogged with books, dolls, and toys.

"You have too many books as it is." Mom's voice was sharp as she left the room.

Chrissy looked wounded at Mom's tone.

"It's not about the book," I explained. "Just like it wasn't about the cookies. Mom's mad at Dad, not at you."

"I don't like them when they fight," she said.

I hugged her. "She tells no lies," I said. "Give the kid a prize."

"Will you teach me to rumpus?" Chrissy asked.

"As soon as I learn," I told her.

Mom's abrupt exit from the bedroom was a bitter contrast to the story time of the good old days. *Get in bed and then I'll come read to you,* Mom would say, the sentence that meant magic would be happening tonight. I'd run upstairs and climb into bed, curl into a nest of pillows, duvet, and stuffed animals. Mom would turn the bedside lamp down low. She wouldn't cuddle in bed with me, but instead sat in a big chair so the circle of light fell on the pages. Mom's voice would drift out of the pale glow as the fairy tales she read came alive. Every character had a different voice. High, low, sneering, sweet, harsh, comical, flutelike, or rolling bass.

The happy memory turned to a shiver as I remembered the night when Mom closed the book and held it against her heart. She had turned the lamp back up, stood, and threw metaphoric ice water onto my warm nest.

"The world doesn't work that way, you know. You don't get rescued. You always have to make your own way."

"I don't want to be rescued, Mom. I just want the prince to come and then I'll be the princess."

"You'd be better off concentrating on being the king," Mom said.

"Women can't be kings," I said.

"Not if they never try," Mom told me.

I wanted to hug her for bringing me the story, and hide under the pillows and cry for taking it all away.

And then she told me I was capable of ruling kingdoms.

She was wonderful. She was cruel. I loved her. I hated her. She was the mystery that was my mother. Now any little soft places she had were hardening.

But had we done anything wrong?

I wanted to rumpus. I wanted to be like those dogs that go crazy in a yard, running up and down along the fence, barking and running and running and barking until they are so tired their tongues hang out and all the crazy is gone.

RUMPUS SCHOOL

Rumpus school was in session as soon as I put a magnet to the window contact. I boosted over the sill and into the totally convenient tree growing next to the house. Dad had even mentioned once that it was a great fire-escape route.

I hit Em's number on Favorites while I was still on the big limb.

"I'm out," I said.

"Cut through the back and meet me a block over in ten. Hide out in that big bush next to the corner."

This covert ops thing already had my adrenaline boosted. A grin pushed its way onto my mouth as I ran, zigzagging for no real reason. I wasn't dodging bullets, but it seemed right to maneuver my way through the dark rather than to walk quietly. I nestled in the leaves of the big bottlebrush-like shrub.

Em pulled up in her mom's car. I got in and she pulled away slow and easy. A serious driver. In control.

"The best way to get a cop's attention is to act like a teenager," she said. "So we don't smoke in the car. It shows our faces too much. We drive like old ladies and we keep to the side streets. Don't drink in the car, even if it's a soft drink. The cops aren't stupid."

"Rumpus school has a lot of rules. You're sounding a lot like Earl."

"Rumpus school? I like that, Tweety. And don't dis Earl. He's the only good husband Mom's had. He acts like he might hang in. If he starts looking like he might bail — I might even straighten up a little to keep him here."

"I'll believe that when I see it," I said.

"Could happen," Emily said. "Now, no guys for

tonight. We need to ease you into rebellion—I mean, rumpusing. Last time you drank and smoked dope you threw up. You don't know when to stop. I'm going to play hall monitor and we'll stick to weed tonight."

Well, if I was going to be a barking dog, I might as well break the law. Going crazy wasn't supposed to be about halfway.

Em drove out of Boulder and found a secluded parking spot that couldn't be seen from the road. Still bundled in our coats, the leather seats with their warmers keeping our rumps cozy, the heater set on toasty for the rest of our bodies, we rolled down the windows a crack so we could let the spruce-scented air drift in and the dope drift out. The satellite radio found a station we agreed on and the music thumped in time with my pulse.

"Open the glove compartment."

A thick baggie full of marijuana and roller papers were front and center.

"I raided Mom's stash. It's the good stuff. That stuff you got sick on was street shit. Mom only smokes the best."

"Your mom...?"

"Oh Ames, wake the hell up. *Your* parents might not now, but trust me, they have. And your grandmom? Give me a break. If I can't find a stash and a bong in her place, I'll kiss your ass at a school assembly."

I handed the baggie to Em and she busied herself rolling a fat doobie. Doobie. I heard that term from Grandmom. She of the Birkenstocks and the Grateful Dead CDs. Hippie holdout stereotype. Rockin' Robin, my dad called her. He was crazy about her. But Mom never even called her mother "Mother." She said that Grandmom never bothered to act like a mother, that she'd wanted to be a "friend."

"Mom always complained"—I made finger quotation marks in the air and mocked my mother's voice—"'Robin has no boundaries. Never gave our lives any *structure*.'"

Em licked the joint, sealing it. "Frankly, I think Robin brought the wrong baby home from the hospital. One of those switched-at-birth things. I can't see your mom sharing any DNA with your grandmom. Seriously." She waved the joint around like a pointer at a blackboard. "Robin's loosey goosey. Your mom is a control freak. Check your pantry. Not one box of oatmeal, but three. Like there's going to be an oatmeal famine day after tomorrow. How many rolls of toilet paper do you have in your house right this minute? Have you *ever* gotten down to the last clean towel?"

I had a flash of my mom's face as she folded and smoothed the thick, fluffy towels, scented with lavender. She always folded and put away the towels herself for some reason, instead of letting Carmen do it.

"I have to admit, if the freezer and refrigerator and pantry aren't full to overflowing, she says someone has to shop before we all starve to death," I said.

Em licked and sealed another joint and handed it over. "Your apple, my friend, didn't fall far from her tree. So shake it off and light up." I leaned forward with the thick, misshapen joint between my fingers, put it between my lips, and drew in as the flame bit the end.

Em lit her joint. "Draw in hard and hold it in," she commanded.

I obeyed. I felt the hot smoke fill my lungs and tingle.

"A few seconds longer," Em warned. I held until I got a head rush, then exhaled. Em was holding her first inhale and she frowned that I hadn't held mine longer. Then she breathed her smoke out like it was a religious experience. "Thanks, Mom," she said.

"My parents are making me insane, Em. My dad loses his job and it's like I find out that..." I stopped, waving my hands as a substitution for words I didn't have.

"You don't know whether to shit or paint your toenails, right?" Em took another drag.

I giggled. I am not a giggler. "Exactly."

"Think about this, Ames. If your mom has to have thirty rolls of toilet paper at any given moment, what do you think is her view on a bank account? On a savings account? Your mom probably just can't deal with money going out and none coming in."

I nodded.

"Take another drag," Em said. I did. "And she's not gonna just take this out on your dad."

"Take what out on him?"

"Your mom is pissed. Your dad isn't doing what she

needs to feel safe. If she doesn't feel safe, she's going to get mean."

"How do you know all this?"

"My mother's been married three times. How many shrinks do you think I've been to?"

"If you're so smart, tell me this. I can't believe this story they're handing me about Dad's job, and I know Dad lied to you about why he drove us to school. So what else have they lied about?"

"Way more than you'd believe. That's what parents do. If it's convenient—they lie. And frankly, Tweety, your parents are a total mystery. I'm not kidding that there were rumors about Witness Protection. It's like you fell out of the sky."

"Huh?"

Emily put up a finger. "A. Family—you don't have any. Well, Robin. But, what do we know about her? Has she ever had a husband? Does your mom have a dad? Where did they live? Your mom doesn't ever talk about it, right?"

"Right," I said. "Who has no other relatives? No aunts,

cousins, nothing. We could have a family picnic with one sandwich." I giggled at my own joke.

Emily put up two more fingers. "Okay, number three..." I thought that was wrong somehow, but my logic was fuzzy. "Your dad. He says your grandparents died in a car accident. Correct?"

"I have been told that is the case," I said, trying to sound like a witness in court.

"Any pictures in your house of them?"

"Nope."

"Don't think that's strange?"

"Not until now. But Mom doesn't have photos displayed. She thinks it's, um..." I raised my nose. "...common."

"So, you've got a weirdo hippie drug grandmom and no, zero, nada other relatives, no pictures, not even photo albums of relatives, no talk about Great Uncle Bernie or cousin Ethel, nothing. Do you know anyone else with a family like that?" Em hooked up an eyebrow in question.

"Oh my gosh, is my dad in the Mafia?" I giggled again.

"I doubt it." Emily took a major drag and held it. Exhaled. Rested. Then said, "But I don't doubt your dad is lying about other people losing jobs. It was just him. And I know because Earl handled something for him. Your dad was his client."

"*What?*" Giggling over.

"Dunno. Earl is closed-mouthed about his work. Lawyer-client privilege and all that. He told Mom your dad's case was complete and that was all he could say. Earl was worried about you and told Mom to keep an eye out..."

Dad, my dad, couldn't be involved in something... *criminal*. Maybe Earl was just doing him a favor.

And yet...

"Until yesterday I felt—I don't know, *safe* somehow. Now..."

"Safe?" Em sucked hard on her joint. "Parents are not there to worry about keeping you safe. It's the three dynamic. Always works against you."

"The what?"

Em slid down in the seat a little. "When there are two

people, they form a bond. Very hard to break. Like you and me. There can't be three best friends. Can't be done. Sooner or later, two will buddy up and turn on the third. In a family, it's almost always the parents against the child. They have the power."

"But—"

"No buts, Tweety. They have secrets. Think, if you want something that's a major purchase, does your mom just hand it over or does she have to 'talk it over' with your dad? They're the adults and are supposed to make major decisions, but don't you feel that a lot goes on behind your back?"

Behind my back. There was plenty going on behind my back right now. "How do you handle it?"

"I pay it back. I put plenty of real estate between me and them. Let them wonder what's going on. I don't depend on them for anything but money and a bedroom."

"Em, if I'm Tweety Bird, right now you feel like Sylvester. I'm tired of flapping around wondering if I'm about to get eaten. I don't want to talk about my parents anymore. I feel like one of those dogs that runs up and down the fence and barks his head off because he can't get out."

Em threw her head back and let loose. "Yip, yip, yip yeeehoooooooooooo!"

What the hell. I howled like a crazy yard dog.

We yipped and bayed and got the munchies and snarfed through the bags of chips and cookies Em had in the back-seat. We sang with the music and cursed our parents, teachers, and every other figure of authority. We giggled down to mellow smiles and figured it was time to roll home. Em's handling of the car was so prudent I think she could teach the Grandma School of Driving.

"Em, a dragonfly just passed us."

"I'm making sure we don't call attention to ourselves."

"Right, you look totally fine. It looks like the car is driving itself."

She dropped me off at the big bush. I boosted myself back up the totally convenient tree and in through my window. As I nestled into my bed, it occurred to me that I had broken all the rules and the world didn't go up in flames. Just a little jog down the dark path, but I had liked it. More than I thought I would.

The rumpus was on.

The next morning my hair and pillowcase reeked of pot. I washed my hair when I showered and opened my window to air out the room. The cologne I sprayed on the pillow didn't help much. But I didn't feel hungover.

I appeared at breakfast, starched blouse buttoned to the neck, hair shiny and combed neatly away from my makeup-free face—the picture of private school–girl correctness. I could have arrived naked and painted blue. Mom stared into her coffee cup, Chrissy ate her pancakes in big-eyed silence, and Dad was AWOL.

I poured a glass of juice and popped a piece of bread into the toaster. Then I clattered the glass and a plate for toast onto the table, neglecting to use a placemat, deliberately trying to rile Mom.

"Daddy's still sleeping. We should be quiet," Chrissy said.

"I couldn't care less if you played the tuba," Mom said. She looked up from her coffee. "He says he can make his own hours now and he's never been a morning person." She took a long look at an empty bottle of Jack sitting on the counter.

"Are you trying to say Dad's hungover?" I leaned across the kitchen table and whispered it. "That bottle could have been almost empty and he just finished it last night."

"It could have," Mom said. "But it wasn't."

My toast popped up. Salvation. The silence was broken by crunching and swallowing and glass clinking, and then Mom stood and grabbed her keys. "Ride with us, Chris."

Usually Chrissy did ride with us because Dad left early for work. Yesterday she stayed with Mom when Dad drove. With Dad home, I guess Chrissy assumed she would wait at home again. Kindergarten didn't start for over an hour.

"Can't I stay with—"

"No, he's asleep. Asleep is not watching. It's not being

responsible." Mom's eyes welled up as she stormed to the car.

At school I realized that I felt way less tense, so less yard dog, than I did at home. I looked forward to having dinner at Em's because I would put off walking into my house, where the air was so heavy, so thick to breathe, that it pushed in from all sides and the top.

When Em's mom picked us up, she gave Em a glare and me a smile. "I'm glad you're coming home with us, Ames. It will take the edge off. Emily's grounded, you know."

Em had told me earlier that she'd been totally busted. Her mom had been sitting on her bed when she got home. She had apparently wanted to sample her own goods and found them missing. Then she found Em gone, and then the car.

Em hadn't busted me, though. That was Em for you. She could get mad at you in a nanosecond, but she never gave you up.

Em's mom loved it that I was Em's best friend. She

thought I was a good influence. My mom was not so enthusiastic, but we'd been friends since we were in play school. We were "new money" and Em's mother was from an "old money" Boulder family. My mom wanted that security that rubbing shoulders with old money provided so she put up with Em's antics for the cachet of the family association.

When we got upstairs, I flopped on Em's bed. "Your groundings are a joke."

"Excuse me," Em said. "I'm a prisoner. I can't leave the house."

"Excuse *me*," I said. "That would be the *mansion*. You can have visitors, use the phone, computer, TV—anything. You just have to entertain yourself at home. With the help of the servants."

"Not called servants. We call them by their names and they are our 'help.' They help us."

"I was grounded once when I was twelve. I was in total solitary confinement. I went to school and went to my room, and my room was stripped of anything but school books and furniture. No communication with the outside world. I even had to eat alone."

"I remember that," Em said. "Wasn't my mom married to the Italian playboy? He called your mom a fascist. I thought that had something to do with skin care. Remind me. Did you, like, kill a priest or something?"

I pitched a silk pillow at Em. "I talked back to my mother."

"Oh yeah. So what would happen if she talked back to *you*?" Em asked.

That side of the picture had never occurred to me.

"You're going to get premature wrinkles," I said. "Change of subject needed."

We headed for Em's computer. "I want to see how many new friends I have." She collected friends on Facebook like her stepfather collected stock options. "Four new ones. Let's see. MonkeyBiznez from Florida, single, male, a little bit kinky. Twenty-six. Hmmm, his taste in music sucks." Em sighed. "Well, he can be a friend but I doubt we'll hook up." She hit the button to accept his friendship offer. "Two from Texas—must have been a slow day in Texas—one from Alaska and one from Japan. Oh, he's cute. Not Japanese, though, his dad's got something to do with the ambassador or something. Cool."

"My dad's from Texas."

"How can I not know that? Stop, of *course* I don't know that. Your family is in Witness Protection."

"I'm starting to think you're right. But he did say he grew up in Texas. I'm not sure even Chrissy knows that. It was a long time ago. He never talks about growing up." I wondered why I never asked Dad about his boyhood. Why hadn't I been interested?

Dinner was quiet, but not uncomfortable. When Em's stepdad is around, it's always quiet. There's something about Earl's presence that makes you want to whisper if you speak at all. I've never seen him in anything but a suit. Ever. But then he's not there much.

When Earl is there, he's totally there. He's not cold or too busy or uninterested or even ultra-businesslike. His presence is, well, calm, reassuring—even peaceful. You don't want to howl at the fence when he's around.

"Ames, it's good to see you."

"Thank you. Are you home for a while?"

He smiled. "Thankfully, yes. I don't have a case outside of Boulder or Denver for six months or more." He winked at Emily. "Em may be feeling a bit confined with my continued presence."

"Earl, you know it's hard to hold a wisp of smoke." Emily waggled her eyebrows. She looked slightly demented.

Amazingly, Earl was amused by Em, and shook his head as if her rebellion were something easily handled. He turned back to me. "Agnes made my favorite dessert. A chocolate chip molten cake. If you have any stress in your life, Ames, one bite will make you forget anything but the magic happening on your taste buds."

"With French vanilla ice cream?" Emily whispered with her eyes shut as if in prayer.

"All of you are going to plump up like Macy's Thanksgiving Day balloons," Em's mother said.

"We'll eat nothing but brussels sprouts tomorrow as an antidote," Earl said.

He said it so solemnly, I believed him until Em rolled her eyes and kicked my shins.

71

Back upstairs Em called her BFM (Boyfriend of the Moment) and I overheard the plans. "Can do. Earl will be driving my friend Ames home. Mom had a megadose of wine with dinner. I can be out the door a little after nine. Mango Tango's great. Don't worry, my ID is foolproof. Kiss, kiss."

"Em, you just got *busted* last night."

"That makes this perfect. They won't think for one minute that I'd try it again tonight." Em stripped off her clothes and put on pajamas. "See, Em knows she's grounded. She's going to watch a movie after her friend goes home. All snug in her little bed."

She threw back her head and made a silent howl.

"You don't look twenty-one. Not even in your slut clothes," I said.

"Doesn't matter. I'm almost sixteen. I'm thinking I need to be arrested at least once before I hit that birthday."

When I got home, Dad was in his study, Chrissy was asleep, and Mom was in bed but surrounded by papers and tapping away at her laptop.

I tried to pass by without speaking, but her radar was up and working.

"Ames, could you come in, please."

"What's up, Mom? Looks like a paper blizzard." I had taken one piece of Em's advice early on. Don't show too much wit to your parents or they'll expect your grades to be better.

"I've taken over the bills from your father while he's looking for work and I'm trying to find ways to cut costs. Honestly, we spend money like drunken sailors."

Mouth moved before head could stop it. "Really? I thought drunken sailors spent money on rum and prostitutes," I quipped, ignoring Em's advice. "What *have* Chrissy and Dad been up to?"

Mom's glare probably stunted my growth. "I don't appreciate this new attitude of yours, Ames. You've been sarcastic and moody. I don't need teen angst along with everything else."

"Everything else *what*? Dad said everything was fine. Nothing would change. You sat right there and didn't argue. Did he lie? Did you?"

Mom looked down at the computer. She pressed her lips together until her mouth was thin and bloodless. "I don't like your shouting, Ames—but I'll answer the question: No, I didn't lie. However, since there is no cash coming in, it seems reasonable to slow the cash going out. Economize a little. That's all. We've let our spending get out of hand."

Mom made a dismissive wave. "Never mind. How was dinner at Em's?"

"She's grounded again for being out late," I lied. "Earl says for her birthday he's going to put a junior lawyer in his firm on retainer for her." That was the truth. He told me that on the way home. I don't think he was joking.

"Yes, well, that's Earl's idea of parenting," Mom said.

My cue to leave. "'Night, Mom." I didn't wait for an answer.

Later I heard Dad come up the stairs. He closed their door and the words of their argument were too muffled to make out.

I turned on my iPhone and stuck in the buds. Tuned out.

* * *

During the first week after his announcement Dad stayed buried in his study, coming out only for dinner. "The chicken is good," he said. "Isn't it?" Dad glanced at me over his wine. "Your mother makes a killer chicken marsala." He didn't look at Mom.

"It *is* good, Mom. You haven't taught me to make this. We should—"

Mom's voice cracked like a dry bone. "Get any leads today, Randal? How many calls did you make?"

Dad finished his glass, then poured another. He took so long to answer I could swear he must be counting his teeth. "I worked on my résumé today. It hasn't been updated in years." He pushed away from his half-finished meal and stood. "Excuse me, Ames, Chrissy, I need to get back to work." He took his wine to his study.

"Ames, you have kitchen duty tonight." Mom slapped her napkin on the table. "I have to have a little personal time." She shoved through the kitchen doors. I knew where she was headed. Personal time meant she would sit at the piano. Mom didn't play. But she loved to sit at the bench, her fingers hummingbirding over the keys, not making a sound, her eyes closed. I guess the symphony was in her head, shoving out the disorder she hated.

The next night and the night after there was no attempt at dinner conversation. After dinner, Mom and I cleaned up and Mom asked, "How was school?"

"Um." I tried to find a mom-friendly way to say that people were avoiding me at school. "Edwin is still trying to trip up our teacher to show off. But he just puts his foot in his mouth and then falls on his face because he can't balance." Nothing from Mom. "But I don't think he's trying to impress me anymore. He doesn't speak to me. Not even hello." Still nothing. "Things are pretty weird at school. I'm feeling kind of—"

"Be careful with that, Ames. You know I don't like you to stack the plates."

Next night: "How was school, Ames?"

"Good, Em is pregnant. Me too. Alien abduction, I'm thinking. But I aced my literature quiz."

"That's excellent."

"That's what I thought you'd say."

Night three I bailed on kitchen duty and followed Dad to his study. I knocked but didn't wait for an invitation to enter. I strode in and sat down in the Chair. The Chair was a leather wingback, big, cushy-soft, kind of cavelike. A family member sat there for the "important" talks. It was a signal. Serious business ahead.

"Okay, spill," Dad said.

"Things aren't fine."

Dad sighed and slumped in his ergonomically correct desk chair. "Not at the moment. True."

I waited.

Dad rubbed his forehead, like he was easing a head-ache. "Things have been a little, um, tense."

"You think?"

Dad grinned and almost, *almost* chuckled. "Sarcasm usually never helps—but just this once..."

Now I grinned.

"Seriously, Ames. This is just a rough patch. Your mother..." He trailed. Sighed. Started again. "You already know Robin and your mother didn't have much money, but you don't know how bad it was. They were poor. Terribly poor. Your mom doesn't talk about it. It embarrasses her. How they had to live. Robin—she never thought that being without money made you poor, so she still doesn't think they were. Your mother is frightened right now. She's afraid—terrified, really—of being poor again."

"She's acting mean, not scared," I said.

Dad turned back toward his computer. "Being mean is easier than admitting you're scared."

I waited for him to say something else, to turn around and hug me or something, anything. I stood up.

"Close the doors on your way out," he said.

Week Two: Looked like the ladies who lunch actually do speak to their daughters (who do not eat actual food at lunch). Kim Banks was rearranging and separating her mixed green salad alphabetically when I sat down. "Have you heard, LayLay? Ames's dad got fired. They are, as my mom puts it, 'Soooo WF.'" In a moment of pity or just to make her spite arrow stick, Kim added, "Without Funds."

"Where did you hear that stupid rumor?" I asked.

"Mom had lunch with Em's mom," Kim said. "Em's mom had the info."

I turned into a statue.

Kim continued. "I guess that means community college for you, Ames. That will keep you close to your *family*." She dinged the last word with a high-pitched, nasal tone, then brayed in laughter.

"Kim, your only shot at Ivy League is if your dad keeps a lawyer on retainer to wipe the coke off your nose before the police find it."

"It's called a trust fund, baby. Too bad you don't have one."

Layla sniffed. "My mom said that she noticed the Fords never have anyone over these days. That's true, notice that, Kim? Reggie?"

Reggie nodded. "I think they have us over once a year and rent furniture for the event. Perfect family, my butt."

"Which appears prominently on the front of your head," Em said as she walked up. "Does it hurt to sit on your face all day?" She turned. "Let's go, Ames." She sniffed the air.

"As Shakespeare once said, 'Me thinketh someone stinketh.'"

We walked to another table. I shook Em off my arm.

"Your mom had lunch with Mrs. Banks and told her my dad was fired?" I shook. Not with anger. I was stunned. How could this be happening?

Em's expression was equally stunned. Then she looked over her shoulder at Kim and the anger flushed. "What comes out of that girl's mouth is exactly what comes out of a pig's ass. Looks, smells, worth the same."

"That's disgusting, Em." I snorted. Relieved. "And I love it."

"My mother had lunch with her mother. That's a fact. But the exchange of information was the other way around. Kim loves to make as much trouble as she can. Because she can."

I now had only one friend. She was a good one.

Week Three: It was late and I was trying to sleep, but sleep must have been out rumpusing. It wasn't in my queen-size canopy bed. I had a gazillion down-filled pillows and I had thumped and fluffed and tried every one of them, but nothing. Was there a pea under my princess mattress? My door edged open a sliver, shut again, then a warm body with cold feet wedged against me.

"Mr. Brown and I need hugs."

I gathered the two hug-starved ones into my arms and squeezed.

"More," Chrissy said.

"Does that mean hug harder or more hugs?"

"Hug longer and more hugs."

"Your wish is my command," I said.

"It's Mr. Brown's wish."

"Does Mr. Brown want to sleep here tonight?"

"I have to ask," Chrissy whispered.

"If he's a smart bear he'll say yes."

Chrissy sighed. "He's always been a smart bear."

I hugged. Longer and more.

The next day I told Mom I was going to Em's after school, but I caught a bus and went to Robin's. She answered my knock.

"It's my favorite grandchild. What are you doing at Dysfunction Junction?"

She held the door wide for me to enter, then kicked the door with the back of her heel while she swooped me into her herb-scented embrace.

When Robin released me I said, "You tell Chrissy that favorite grandchild thing, too. I'm on to your tricks, Grandmom."

Robin wore one of her three shapeless dresses made of hemp. Her skin, free of makeup, was still soft and smooth, except for the smile lines around her mouth and eyes.

"You teaching the old ladies anything new?"

"Phooey, the old ladies are at the clubhouse with their codger husbands. Can't teach any of them a thing."

When Dad bought our Boulder house he bought Robin a small condo in a retirement community. I know he paid cash for it, because Grandmom didn't want to take it and he said it was a done deal. She told him it was a good thing it wasn't in a gated community or he couldn't have gotten her in it with a catapult.

"Have you been cheating those old folks at poker again, Grandmom?"

"I don't have to cheat. They're so busy talking about their latest bowel movement or their next surgery that they don't know what's in their hand. I have no remorse over taking a fool's money."

How could anyone not love Grandmom Robin?

Mom didn't.

"You didn't come here to tell me how good-looking I am," Grandmom said. "So — it's got to be — yup, that's it. It's high time for boy problems. I was wondering when some boy would break your heart or, more likely, you'd be dragging your feet because you're afraid he might."

Somehow I found myself in a chair with a cup of chai tea on the table in front of me. I wanted to tell her about Dad, his job, Mom, Chrissy, but...now, it seemed... disloyal, or...like it would be loading my problem onto Robin.

"Wrong. Not a boy. It's Mom."

Grandmom sat in a chair across the small, round

kitchen table from me. It was one of those tiny chrome things that looked like it came out of a '50s diner. Not a new retro, this one had a Dumpster rehab look. She put her mug of chai down. "You two butting heads like a couple of mountain goats again?"

"Sort of. Dad told me that I need to understand her. That she's scared of being poor."

"Randal said that, did he?" She picked up her cup and sipped. "That's true."

"So, how poor were you? Why is she like this?"

"We had everything we needed. When your mother was young we had adventures. We saw this country from the swamps, to the deserts, to the mountains, and a few skyscrapers." Grandmom smiled but not at me; she was caught in memory. "We met storytellers and poets and artists and fools and tramps and kings and a few saints. I was never so happy."

Grandmom came back to Dysfunction Junction. "I wish I could take you on a journey like that."

"Why don't you?"

"Your mother said that if I didn't learn to lead a

'normal' life I couldn't be around you or your sister. She thought I'd be a bad influence."

"Mom blackmailed you? With this condo?"

"No. Randal gave this to me. So I could be close." Her words were right. Her tone wasn't.

"Then why does Mom think she was poor?"

"That's her story to tell."

"Mom is barely decent to you. How can you love her?"

"I do. I love her completely. Understand her? No."

Grandmom Robin patted my hand. "Love's not always rosebuds and bluebirds, my girl." She shook her head. "No, love can be a wicked thing."

Week Four: Mom went from stressed to wired to the snapping point. Dad was always home when I returned from school. He didn't eat with us. I don't know for sure if he slept upstairs with Mom or not. He was up there in the morning when I awoke, but Mom was in the kitchen by then. Today, I would try again to get my dad to be my dad again. I missed him.

I tapped on the glass of the French doors and entered. "Hey, Dad. What's up?"

He tapped his keyboard. "I'm working," he snapped. Then he stretched his arms over his head and cricked his neck. "Sorry—deep in thought and all that. You startled me."

"How's it going?"

"What?" It was just one word, but I swear, if you can be guilty and suspicious at the same time, that's just how my dad sounded.

"Job search? Any leads? Interviews maybe?"

He took a long swig from his glass of Jack. "Stop nagging; you sound like your mother." He turned back to his computer.

It felt like a slap in the face. "I guess that would be a *no*." I whisked out of the room and let the doors slam shut behind me.

One afternoon in early March, Chrissy was in her room mushing Play-Doh through a plastic figure. The Play-Doh made hair.

"Look, the elephant has pink and green hair."

"Like all good elephants," I said. "How was school today, Missy Chrissy?"

"Didn't go."

"You didn't go? Are you sick?"

"Nope, Mommy called my school and said I'm not going there anymore. I'm going to go to another kindergarten starting Monday. We won't have to pay for me twice, Mom said."

"Public school. Did she say you were going to public school?"

"That's it. She and Daddy yelled real loud. Private school costs too much money and we already pay for public school." Chrissy nodded.

Wow, this was big.

"She called your school, too," Chrissy said.

"*What?*"

"Mom's face got red when she talked on the phone. Then she told Daddy that they wouldn't give back the money. They paid for the..." Chrissy looked up, searching.

"Semester," I offered.

"Right. That. It didn't matter where you went to school, they couldn't get the money back."

"Did they say I'd have to change schools in September?"

"Mom did, but Dad got real mad and said he'd have a new job by then and they kept fighting. Mom threw a bunch of papers at him and said, 'These bills won't wait 'til September.'"

Was this what Dad's idea of "fine" looked like?

That evening Mom had more economizing in store.

"Ames, I've canceled your iTunes account," Mom said.

"What? Why?" I asked.

"Because last month alone you downloaded fifty-seven dollars' worth and this month you already have thirty-six dollars pending," Mom snapped. "What are you thinking?"

"I'm thinking that downloading's much cheaper than buying the CD. Didn't you just say we needed to economize?"

"Ames, do you really not get this? I've canceled your Amazon account, too."

"I'm not supposed to read?"

"Libraries are full of books. Use them. I see you ordered a book for Chrissy that I told her she couldn't have."

"You were mad at Dad and taking it out on her." I stood up. "Dad said nothing would change."

"Watch your tone, Ames."

"I feel like I'm being set up," I said. "You tell me none of this will touch us. Nothing will change. And then when I do what I've always done — act like nothing has touched us — I'm the bad guy. That's just crap."

"Ames, go to your room," Mom commanded.

"That's where I'm fucking going."

Chrissy gasped and Mom looked at me like a stranger stood in front of her.

I turned and heard Chrissy's voice waver like she was about to cry. "Mom?"

"Don't worry, sweetie. Everything is fine," Mom said.

I went upstairs to the media room. Two rows of over-stuffed chairs stadium-style in a room with no windows in front of a wall-to-wall television. I popped in one of Dad's car-chase-fifteen-bodies-mangled-before-opening-credits action movies. Mom barged in. "Turn that off."

"I'm watching it." I was determined she wouldn't get a reaction from me.

She grabbed the remote and punched it.

"You're grounded. No TV, no movies, no nothing."

"Big whoop."

"I want your iPhone."

"You can't do that!" I bolted to my feet. So much for no reaction.

"Watch me. Do you know our cell phone bill is over four hundred dollars a month?"

"My music is on my phone. My pictures and texts and e-mail."

"All of that is on your laptop."

"Like I can carry around my laptop listening to my music?"

"Get an after-school job. Earn your iPhone."

"I'm not sixteen. You can't work until you're sixteen. It's like child slavery or something."

Mom sighed and rolled her eyes. "Don't be such a drama queen. You can babysit. Sell some of these clothes on eBay. You're clever. Think of something. That's what I'm doing."

We stood staring at each other for a moment. I had never before had this feeling of wanting to land a full-on slap across my mother's mouth.

Then Mom swiveled around and strode to my room. I launched after her and saw her snatch the phone off my bed.

"Can't you cancel the wireless and calling plan and leave me the iPhone? I could still use it for my music and pictures. Without the connection I can't download anything that costs money."

"That would have been fine if you hadn't acted like a spoiled brat. You need to learn to deal. Life is not going to be what it was. Your princess days are over."

Mom elbowed past me and slammed my door.

I sat on the bed. I hadn't thought about this. What couldn't we pay for? No vacations? Fine. No new clothes? Not fine, but okay. No new...stuff? Bad, but we'll live.

I hated the no-phone part, but...I'm thinking it doesn't stop there.

Without Funds.

What does that mean?

Were we poor? The kind of poor I watched on TV where people lived in boxes on the street? Or just the kind of poor where you lived all crunched up together in a little apartment in a crappy neighborhood? Were we the kind of poor that had no car at all or some old beater that had rust spots, or maybe a decent-looking used station wagon? Would I have to cut my own hair? Would we even have enough food to eat?

I didn't know how to be poor. I know it sounds snotty as all hell, but I knew already that being poor would eat me up and spit me out.

There was no chat driving to school the next morning. Mom didn't even bother to say hello to Em. I couldn't wait to get to school.

I wasn't going to do any work as long as I was grounded. I'd have to ask Em how to be a class washout. But then,

Em always managed to pull an abracadabra and yank her grades into shape at the last minute. The girl was a magician.

"I called last night and your cell phone service is canceled," Em said, like someone had chopped off my leg.

"Yep. Monster Mom took the phone, and I've lost my iTunes and Amazon accounts, the works, and I'm grounded for two weeks because I have a bad attitude."

"This is serious. She has never canceled your phone."

"I know, she says it's all about economizing. Like a fifty-dollar iTunes bill will make a difference." I stopped. "You know what? I think she's fired Carmen. I haven't seen her in a couple of weeks."

Em nodded. "She did. Carmen is working for Naomi's mom on Tuesdays and Thursdays now." Long. Uncomfortable. Pause. "Earl said something weird last night."

I didn't want to hear what Em would say next.

"My mom's still poking around for information. She managed to get Earl to slip up and say that he helped your dad work out a deal with his company. He said that your dad's lucky not to have ended up in jail over it."

I closed my locker, then leaned my face against it. "Jail?"

"That's all I know. I swear. He got up and told my mom not to ask him another question. That what he already said was unethical." Em studied her shoes. "I thought about not telling you. I figured your parents hadn't. You need to know before you get blindsided with it from people that don't love you." She scrutinized me and I looked away. "You okay? Want to bail and talk it through?"

I didn't want to talk. I couldn't even think. I shook my head. "Thanks, but later."

Em didn't say anything. She turned and left.

I dream-walked that day. The only answer I had for any teachers was "I don't know." The only word in my head was "jail."

Jail?

Mom and Dad were in full-scale combat mode when I interrupted them in Dad's study that evening. Mom was shoving papers under Dad's nose and Dad was pushing them away. They were screaming over each other.

"Stop. There's a child in the next room!" I yelled.

They turned and all the fury they had for each other zeroed in on me.

"You know not to come in here if the door is closed," Dad said.

"You can add another week—" Mom began.

"To my grounding. I think we're past that. Please, can we go back in time to when you used to tell me the truth? Or have you always lied to me?"

They looked like small animals caught in traps.

I decided to go for the jugular. "Jail. What did you do to deserve it, Dad, and how did you avoid it?"

Any hope that Em's drama-queen proclivity had been at work here took the big flit when Dad's head drooped like a flower on a broken stem.

Mom sat, prim and quivering on the leather couch. "I told you we couldn't keep this a secret."

"Dad?" I demanded.

He stood and approached me. "It's not your concern, Ames. It's mine and I'll take care of everything. It's all going to be—" He reached out as if to put his hand on my shoulder.

"*Fine?*" I loaded my voice with contempt and stepped back from his touch. "Sorry, but our house has become a war zone, you've been lying to me for weeks, my sister is in public school now and I'll be there in September, my phone is gone, but the big news—the headline—is that my father barely skidded past the *go directly to jail* square. And other people knew it first. What kind of bullshit is this? Tell me how I'm supposed to *listen* to you? Let alone *trust* you?"

I slammed out of Dad's study. I heard the French door hit and bounce back against the wall.

I turned to see an ugly crack splitting through the leaded and beveled glass. Ruined.

That dark thrill, like the opening bars of a discordant song, flickered in me. I could hurt things. It frightened me. It made me feel like all my pulse points pounded in rhythm to that new, mysterious beat.

It took Dad an hour to search out the courage to enter my room.

"Don't sit on my bed," I said without looking up from my journal.

He sat in the fluffy chintz chair that tucked into the makeup table directly opposite. He kept his back to me, his head hanging, a full glass of Jack in his hands. He took a breath and launched in, speaking to the mirror that hung on the wall over the table.

"I was taking money from customers' accounts and using it to buy short. You can make a killing like that. You put the money back in the accounts, and they never know." He glanced away from my mirror image, seemingly speaking to his drink. "Then the whole economy nose-dived, and the numbers went against me. I couldn't put the money back. It was okay at first. Nobody looks at those accounts but once a year at audit time, so I kept trying to play catch-up, drawing bigger amounts from other accounts. I made a few of the big draws up, but..."

His voice caught and so he took a gulp from the glass. "I got caught. I wasn't *downsized*, I was fired. I had to pay back what I could out of my retirement. There's no settlement money. Em's dad persuaded them to avoid the scandal and not press charges. I can't get a recommendation. Hell, no one will even interview me."

I wavered between the need to hug him and kick his butt. I couldn't stand the self-pity and he had done so much that was so wrong, but—he was my dad. He was my dad. My voice softened and I swear, I *swear* I was gentle as I said the words.

"Get a job doing something else. You screwed up. Take it on the chin." I turned to look at him. The glass behind him was empty.

Dad walked over to the bed and scowled at me. "You sound just like your mother. I'm good at what I do, Ames. If I take some low-paying temp job, I'll never get a corporate job again. I know how these things work." I could smell the Jack on his breath and his face was red and strained.

"I guess you want me to trust you on that," I said.

He lifted his hand, palm open ready to slap me. I gasped, bracing for the strike.

It didn't come. The utter betrayal had already hit me, though.

Dad looked at his hand as if he was surprised to see it there. He lowered it, looking ashamed and confused.

When he left the room he didn't close the door.

The only reason I knew I hadn't turned to stone was that I felt Chrissy's warmth as she snuggled in next to me in bed that evening.

"Stay here. You make me feel better," I told her.

Chrissy nestled in tighter. "My room is next to theirs and I can hear them fight at night. It makes my bears nervous when they do that. It's a lot worse now than it was before."

I let that lay still in the room for a minute.

"Before? You heard Mom and Dad fighting a lot *before* he lost his job?"

"Lots."

"You never told me," I said.

Chrissy didn't answer. But I knew. I hadn't asked. Chrissy was like a tape recorder, full of information, but you had to punch the right button for playback.

"What did they fight about?"

"I don't know. I couldn't hear the words good, just the angry."

Just the angry. That's all that was left in this house. The angry.

"Did Daddy hit you?" she asked me out of the blue. I was stunned. I hadn't known she'd caught any of that scene through the open door to my room.

"No, but he wanted to. He almost did," I said.

"Why?"

"He was mad at me because I wouldn't let him lie anymore. And he was mad at Mom and, I don't know, maybe he's mad at the whole world."

"D'you think he'll try to hit me someday, too?"

I closed my eyes and tears leaked out and ran back toward my ears. I pulled one hand from behind my head and curled it around Chrissy. "No. I will never, ever let anyone hurt you."

It used to be that home was my warm, safe nest. Then school became my refuge. Now, the social parts of school were toxic and the classroom stuff seemed like my only place to get peace. This morning Edwin was Bivens-baiting again, and it set my head spinning. When Mr. Bivens got the class settled, I couldn't make sense of the work. Numbers, letters, signs, sines. They hopped around like fleas on a dog's back. I couldn't keep still. I drummed my pencil, I crossed and recrossed my legs. I wrote, erased, sighed, looked out the window, at the clock, around the room.

When the bell rang I walked straight out of school and to the nearest Starbucks. I had enough money to get even more wired on Sumatra and read newspapers the rest of the day.

I didn't go home until I figured Mom, Dad, and Chris would be having dinner. I was sloshing with coffee and too mad to eat so I banged in the kitchen door, was up the stairs and locked inside my room before they could register my presence.

Mom banged on my door. "Let me in here this minute. You skipped out after your second class."

"If you ground me at night, I'll take my free time during the day."

"Ames."

"Go away."

Oh yes, we were a pretty family now. Let's put on the

101

reindeer antlers and take the Christmas photo. Paste on the cheesy smile like we do in those portraits Mom had taken for our holiday cards, posed in August so the best photographer in Boulder could fit us in. Sweaters and artificial snow.

I knew Mom was still listening outside my door, wondering what to say to me.

"Go *away*, Mom. There're things we shouldn't say to each other right now."

When I got up, I found a note from Mom: *If you plan to go to school, you can use the bus or ask Em to take you. I'm done with chauffeuring you.*

So I guess Mom didn't care if I went to school anymore. I phoned Em.

"I've been waiting here by the phone for you, Tweety. What's the drama at your house? Your mom called and told my mom that your attitude has put you on your own and she's not carpooling."

"I hooked out yesterday, told Mom that I wasn't listening to her anymore, and this is her payback."

"No worries. I'll bat my eyes and sweet-talk Mom and she'll feel sorry for you. She thinks people that ride city buses carry infectious disease. She won't let you die of the wikizooties or anything."

Soon, Em and her mom pulled into the drive and I dashed out.

"Ames, your mother is under a lot of stress," her mom reminded me, as if I didn't know. "You just have to be understanding. I know it feels awful right now. Let her calm down. Don't worry about school. We'll be glad to run you back and forth until your mother gets her feet back under her."

"Thanks."

Get her feet back under her. I hated those stupid sayings. Her feet weren't going to get back under her as long as they were all over *me*.

WHEN THE ROBIN ROARS

When I walked into the kitchen that afternoon, Grandmom Robin was pacing the floor, holding a rolling pin like a lethal weapon. Mom, Dad, and Chrissy were sitting in the kitchen chairs like scolded children. Grandmom pointed to the vacant chair and I sat down. It struck me how scary it was to greet Grandmom and to have her respond without a smile.

"Isn't this a charming bunch? I have to hear from a bawling six-year-old that my son-in-law is a 'robber' who might be smacking his teenage daughter around. That my daughter has turned into Shylock where nothing seems to matter but the almighty dollar. My oldest granddaughter compounds the situation by offering boatloads of nothing but trouble." She stopped, crossed her arms over her chest, and surveyed us. "Does that about cover it?"

There was a beat or two of silence, and then chaos as everyone started talking at once. Mom shouted at Robin, Dad shouted at me, I shouted at Chrissy, and Chrissy sobbed into the neck of her favorite bear.

Robin smacked the table top with the rolling pin. "Hush!" Dad and I jumped back in our chairs and Chrissy sobbed harder. Mom just glared.

Grandmom's voice rose. "You've made the only sane person in the room cry. Not another word." Her hair had come loose from its messy bun and the wisps around her head made her look wild. The set of her mouth was threatening. Where was my mellow grandmom Robin?

"Consider this an intervention," she said. "Because you people are totally messed up."

"Robin, you're one to be talking…" Mom started.

"Okay, that makes you first. Why are you screaming at your children? What are you so afraid of? This isn't the end of the world."

Mom's mouth dropped open. "Do you think I'm supposed to go back to living in a tent again? Raise my girls in a park panhandling while I tell bogus fortunes with Tarot cards?" Her hands had curled into fists. "You think this isn't the end of the world?"

Robin's face softened. "That was over twenty years ago...for two months. It was an adventure, Diana."

"An *adventure*? I grew up with my stomach in knots from the uncertainty. You think life isn't about money, it's about love and freedom and all that babble. It *is* about money. Money is safety." Her voice dropped and she arranged and rearranged the salt and pepper shakers. "Ames here seems to think I don't remember what it's like to be a teenager. Well, I remember. I remember being frightened every minute. Scared to sleep, thinking that some drug-crazed man would snatch me out of a tent. Embarrassed that I had to use the public restrooms. Mortified when I couldn't get a shower or a clean towel." Mom's voice cracked.

"So the situation you're in now is my fault?" Robin's voice was softer but gave no ground. "Once you got that great job and married a man who made wads of cash, you still couldn't take the reins of your own destiny?"

"I did, until he destroyed it." Mom's voice was poisonous.

"Okay, you put your life in a man's hands and he messes up. What happens now?" She jerked the salt and pepper shakers away so Mom couldn't obsess over them. "It looks like you're just going to shout at people and blame anyone that gets in your crosshairs."

Mom deflated a little. "Why is this all on me? I didn't do this."

"It isn't all on you," Robin said. "But you're still on your ass. Do you have a plan to get off it?"

Robin got herself a glass of water and turned her attention to Dad. "Now, as for you: You stole from your clients? You have no job and no hope of getting another one?"

Dad refused to look at Grandmom. "Look at me and tell me I don't have a grasp of the situation?"

"I've worked hard all my life to give this family the best—"

"You also gave Diana false confidence in your finances. You pushed to buy this house and you pushed her to leave her job. You gambled with money you didn't have. That leaves you with no excuses. So if you need to move, you'll move. If you need to work a blue-collar job, you'll do that. If Diana divorces you..."

Dad tightened his jaw.

"I'd kick you out before you could fart or spit, but knowing her, she's going to torture you instead. If she does divorce you, you'll find work and you'll support your children or the courts won't need to find you. Do you understand me, Randal?"

Dad looked like something was eating him from the inside out. Then, Robin turned to me.

"You're being the whiny rich kid playing poor pitiful me, acting out by boosting out of windows at night. Aren't you a big help?"

"They *lied*," I accused, hearing the whine in my own voice.

"You don't?" Robin shot back. "You act like this family was the perfect Kodak snapshot before. That's one big lie, too."

I sat back in my chair. "That's not true."

"Ames, I love you, but you live in your own world. You've been spoiled from day one. Think about it. You wanted what you wanted, and you wanted it now."

"All little kids are like that," I said.

"Is Chrissy?" Robin drummed her fingers on the table. I looked at Chrissy. No, she wasn't.

"Grandmom, where's Rockin' Robin?" I asked, almost in a daze. "You're as bad as *she* is."

"Ames!"

I wanted to smile at how insulted Mom sounded.

Robin grabbed my hand. I tried to shrug her off but she held on too tight. "How did you get this angry? The world has always been so easy for you. Is that why you feel so betrayed?" Robin's voice was gentler than her grip. "You are your mother made over, Ames."

"I'm nothing like my mother." I darted a look. Mom's mouth was set in a line and her eyes were ice.

Grandmom paused, then shook her head. "Could the rest of you go to the living room. See if you can work on a plan of action that might get you off your backsides." Chairs scraped back. Mom put each one carefully back in their place, and then she followed Dad and Chrissy out.

"Think again, Ames. Remember going to see Jimmy Buffett on my birthday? Remember how you didn't need a towel?" She left the kitchen and went into the living room, leaving me to linger over her puzzle.

A couple of years ago, for her birthday, we took Robin to see Jimmy Buffett playing an outdoor concert in Denver. We were heading to the car for the drive down and it started pouring. Mom ran inside to check all the windows so nothing would get ruined. I hauled butt for the car so I wouldn't get wet. The goofy threesome, Robin, Dad, and Chrissy, stood there like turkeys with faces turned to the rain, getting drenched, sticking their tongues out, arguing about what the rain tasted like.

Then I got Robin's point: Mom came out of the house

with three towels, like she knew only three of us would need them. But not me. She knew I'd never stand out in the rain getting soaked if I didn't have to. Like her.

Something dangerous reared its head. *I'm nothing like her.*

I walked into the living room. Robin gestured me to a chair. "Now, what's the plan?" she asked.

"Randal and I both look for jobs," Mom said. "They won't be the pay grades or the prestige we're used to, but we'll have to get past that."

Dad seemed to be sucking his cheeks to the inside of his mouth, but he nodded.

"Can you keep up the mortgage on this house?"

Sweat popped out on Dad's brow. "No."

Mom closed her eyes for a long minute, then opened them again. "We have some high ticket items here that'll sell quickly. That should cover us for a month or two. We put the house on the market tomorrow and look for a cheaper place, hopefully in a decent school district for Ames and Chrissy, since they'll go to public school."

Robin nodded. "There's an age limit for my condo and a no-children clause, so you can't move in with me, but I'll put it on the market right away."

"You can't," Dad muttered.

"Randal?" Mom asked.

"Deed is in my name so I could pay the taxes. I took a second mortgage on it. I owe back taxes. You're going to lose it, Robin."

"Good." Robin didn't bat an eye. "I hate the place. Too many old people."

I stared at Dad. "Dad! How could you *do* that to Grandmom?"

"Ames, I'll be fine. I could survive in a tin can. That's the difference between the Fords and me." Robin gestured to Mom. "Diana, stop shooting black looks at your husband. You had a plan. Keep talking."

Mom worked her jaw back and forth. She took a couple of deep breaths and continued. "Since the house we move to will be smaller we can sell quite a bit of furniture and art, we might take a beating on this house, but we should have enough for a decent down payment and a little savings. It will be a different life, but it's what we have to do."

"Randal, are you on board?" Robin's voice was not friendly.

"I said yes, didn't I?" He shoved back his chair and went to the kitchen. He came back with a Corona. "You have my word. Do you need my testicles for collateral?"

"Like you have any," Mom said under her breath, quick as a snake bite.

"Diana! Divorce him or welcome him into the boat. Use the oars to row, not to beat each other over the head. Ames, what about you?"

I looked at Dad, Mom, and Robin. Finally at Chrissy. I thought about Mom at thirteen, homeless and scared.

"I'm on board. No spending. No boosting out windows. I'll go to public school. I won't give anyone attitude. But I want to be in the boat, too. Don't lie to me. Tell me what's really happening. That's all I want," I said.

I could see by Robin's glance that she wasn't sure she believed me.

Now that Mom had a plan, an outline, rules, a checklist, she was easier in her skin. She got her laptop and typed and tapped. I assume since she was moving from room to room and surveying before she typed that she was making a list of salable items.

"Mom, what can Chrissy and I help you do?"

"At this stage, not a lot. You can get Chrissy ready for bed, you can do your homework without a fuss. I'm going to be busy sorting things and looking for a house and getting this one ready for sale, all while looking for a job. You'll have to take up the slack around here." Mom sighed. "I'll make out a chore sheet for each of you tomorrow."

The Commander was back.

THE OARS AREN'T
FOR ROWING

When I stepped out of Em's car the next day, six burly
men were transferring our grand piano into a truck. The
piano was wrapped and packaged and the legs were
removed and I guess already in the truck, so that it looked
like a puffy kidney that weighed a gazillion pounds.

"Oh," Em's mom exhaled. Pity. Clear and undisguised.
We were garage-sale poor.

"You win!" Em shouted. "No more piano lessons.
Awesome."

"I haven't had piano lessons in years, Em," I reminded her—like I was justifying this whole embarrassment. I cringed.

"We'll see you tomorrow, Ames, sweetie," Em's mom said. *Sweetie*. I cringed again. I was climbing the pity ladder fast.

I walked through the kitchen and looked into the formal living room. Mom was lingering in the great big hole of space, absently toeing the imprints in the carpet left from the piano legs. She looked like somebody had skinned her cat.

"I hate this," I said.

Mom puffed her cheeks full of air, then let it out of her mouth like a balloon deflating. "I never saw anyone with a piano living in a tent," she murmured, almost as if to herself. She put her fingertips against her lips.

I stepped close and put my arms around Mom to hug her. She jerked back, surprised at my touch. "I can't deal with anything else right now, Ames. Anyone else. Please, go away. Go watch TV or something." Mom returned to rubbing out the carpet indentations.

I knew she was hurting. But the first time I tried to help row, Mom swatted me with her oar.

I headed to Chrissy's room. "C'mon, small-type person," I said when I found her in the closet rearranging her bears. "I'm inviting you and one bear of your choice to watch TV or a movie, also of your choice. I draw the line, however, at any purple character or talking unicorns. And I'm not too fond of mermaids."

"You'll watch a whole movie with me?"

"Abso-certain-lutely."

"That's not a real word," Chrissy said.

"Is now," I said. "What do you think about tacos for supper? I'm going to cook tonight," I said.

"You can cook?" Chrissy asked.

"We'll have to see," I said.

There were talking bears in the movie. Haven't a clue what they talked about but Chrissy recited the dialogue with them and Mr. Brown clapped a lot. When the movie finished and we opened the door we heard the sounds of an argument drifting up the stairs. I was halfway down when I could make out the words.

"I don't *believe* you!" It was Mom shouting. "You lazy piece of *crap*. How *could* you?"

"For one single minute, can you not nag and scream in my ear? Just sell everything I worked to give you and shut the hell up," Dad roared back.

"Back to your room," I told Chrissy. "You need to guard your bears while I try to calm things down."

Chrissy put her hands over her ears and ran back up the stairway and then to her room. She slammed the door behind her.

When I got down to the first floor, I saw Mom towering over Dad as he sat at his desk, shouting at her and pouring a drink. A computer card game was on the computer screen. I listened and put what bits I understood together.

Mom had walked in on Dad while he was playing computer poker and she'd lost it. Why wasn't he looking for a job, doing his share? This was all his doing; it was his responsibility to make it right. Rinse and repeat.

Dad: How many hours a day can I search for jobs

online? If you can spend an hour sobbing over a piano and toeing carpet marks, why can't I have fifteen minutes to play a game to de-stress? My money bought the piano that you just sold; that's my contribution for the day — where's yours?

Each just wanted to win. The oars weren't meant to move the boat forward. They were weapons.

They hadn't kept their word for one day. Not a single day.

I had to get out of here before I physically hurt someone.

I grabbed the phone in the kitchen and dialed Em. "Can we get to the mall?"

"Sure. Have you met my new guy? He's a cowboy. He's eighteen so he can take us. Be outside in ten."

I was outside in ten and in the long-legged, slow-talking boy's backseat in ten and a half.

"Ames, this is Win."

"Pleased to meet you," Win said.

"Win? Short for something?" I asked.

"Lord, yes. Something long and tongue-tangled and got some Roman numerals, too. We'll just keep it at Win, if you don't mind."

"Secrets, lies, and theft, that's my life now," I said.

"Well, little missy," Win said to Em. "I thought you were the sassy one of this bad-girl team."

"I need to learn. I'm poor now and I think shoplifting might become a necessary skill."

"Wait a minute. Do you want to start shoplifting to piss off the parents and get a little payback—show them you can lie and steal, too? Or are you shoplifting to get stuff you can't afford now?" Em asked.

"Could be both," I said.

"*So* not true. But it's good enough. What are you after? New cell phone?"

"I don't think so," Win countered. "You can lift the phone, but you have to pay for the plan. That gets complicated. Now, I might know some people..."

"Nah, I just want an iPod for now."

"Easy peasy."

*　　　*　　　*

When I slid the iPod into my purse and turned toward the door, I felt that dark thrill, that silver cool feeling of deceit and being something I had never been.

But Apple was on the ball and we were busted before we were halfway out the door. Our tears and *it was just a joke*—sort of a dare—like a scavenger hunt—*we're so sorry*'s fell on totally deaf ears. It didn't help that I had wire cutters in my pocket.

Mall security turned us over to the police, who hauled our butts downtown. We were printed, photographed with a digitally entered numbered sign just like in the movies. We were searched, humiliated, and slapped in a cell. Because we were juvies they put us in a cell together and not with adults. The cowboy got adult treatment, but he looked like he was used to the drill.

"What about our call?" Em demanded.

"You watch too much TV," the officer said. "You're juveniles. You don't get a call. I call your parents. Go sit down."

"So what do you think of jail?" Em whispered, nodding across to the big holding tank at the jeering, trash-talking pros in ho outfits and vomiting women who had been without drugs a little too long.

I flashed back to how the word *jail* had sent ice down my spine when Em first said it in relation to my dad.

"I'd rather be here than home," I said.

"Wow, things are really circling the drain for you, aren't they?"

I sat on the stainless steel "bed." Sighed.

In an hour, Em's stepdad, in his perfect suit and his tightly knotted silk tie, appeared. "Let's go."

"Earl, when you leave Mom, please take me with you," Em said.

I still sat on the bed. "You too, Ames," Earl said. "All arranged. You're released to my custody."

"That was fast," Em remarked.

"I only play golf because the judges do," he shot back.

"Are my parents out there?" I asked.

Earl scowled. "You'll be staying with us tonight, Ames. We'll discuss that at the house. Let's get you out of here."

We signed for our things. Earl did some business and we were in the backseat of his car.

"Em, will you understand when I tell you that you're an idiot?" her stepdad asked.

"I'd understand and agree, Earl," Em replied.

"Sir, this was all my fault," I broke in. "I asked Em to do this with me."

"That's probably true, Ames, except that I suspect you asked Em to show you how. Am I correct?"

"I needed a new iPod. My mom took mine."

"Never lie to your lawyer. That can't be the only reason. Em has a handful of those things she could lend or give you." A short silence. "Ames, I know why Em shoplifts—it's her head rush. She's also savvy enough to know that everything on her record before she's eighteen is sealed. She knows what real trouble is and how to stay out of it. She flirts with trouble but she doesn't kiss it." Em laughed, but my head spun. "I think it's different with you."

I thought for a minute.

"I guess...I just wanted to see how it felt to steal." Never lie to your lawyer, I reminded myself. "To do— something...bad, I guess."

"How'd that work out for you?" Em's stepdad asked.

I didn't reply. Earl wouldn't approve of the honest answer.

It felt dangerous. I found something dark in me that sang. I wanted to listen. Maybe I wanted to sing, too.

When we got back to Em's, Earl told her to go up to her room and get ready for bed. "I need some time with Ames."

Em's face turned totally serious and suddenly she was all good-girl behavior. She slid out of the seat, through the door from garage to house without a word.

Earl put his arm on the back of the seat and turned so he could face me. "I'll represent you in this shoplifting case. Since you didn't make it out of the store, nothing was stolen, so it boils down to attempted shoplifting. It will be taken care of in tandem with Em. It's easily handled." He stopped. I think he was waiting for me to say something. His silence sounded lawyerly.

"This isn't like you, Ames." He nailed me with a steady look. "I never picked your father to embezzle from his clients. Now you steal just to see what it feels like?

"Ames, I am sympathetic, but you are in trouble on so

many levels. More than legal. When I called your house to get your father or mother to come with me to get you out of jail..." Again with the drilling look. "Your father was too drunk to drive and your mother said that she couldn't deal with you. I told her that I would take care of everything."

Finally, someone told the truth. My mother and father didn't give a shit. They were too absorbed in their own miserable worlds.

Tears pushed their way to my eyes. I blinked and fought them back.

"Ames, I'm not sure they would have left you in jail, but...I'll be here for you if I can. Circumstances being what they are, however, you need to stay out of trouble." He stopped. "I wish I could do more to help you, but...the law won't allow me to do much." He appeared frustrated. I had never seen Earl frustrated. He drummed his fingers on the seat back. "You need to stop acting out. You don't have the liberty to rebel like a normal teen right now. I was here to catch you this time, but next time you fall, I might not be around."

Translation: Get used to being unprotected.

*   *   *

When I got to Em's room, she had pajamas on the bed for me. I showered first, washing jail off my skin and out of my hair with hot water and tea tree oil shampoo. I came out of the bath feeling less of a felon but more of an orphan. Chinese takeout was sitting in white boxes in Em's sitting room.

"Let's take this stuff to the media room and watch a movie," Em suggested.

"Works for me," I said. We ferried the stuff down the hall and settled in.

"I get kicked out and you get takeout. What's with that?"

"You're carrying my weight here. Earl and Mom feel so sorry for you that they kind of forgot I got arrested. By the time they remember, they won't be nearly as mad as they would have been." She flipped through the DVDs. "Something stupid-type funny?"

"Sounds right."

Em slid in a DVD and hit the remote. "Let's see what Mom ordered." She sorted through the boxes. "Sweet and sour shrimp. Yum." She handed me a plate and chop-sticks.

"My life has turned to crap," I said. It was matter of fact. No whine, no anger. Just that hard-to-find element: truth.

"It's looking that way. Seriously, I'm not going to blow smoke up your butt on this one. Your dad should be in prison, your mother is selling all your stuff, and they were going to leave you in jail. This is not good."

I couldn't argue.

"All for ditching school once and getting busted for trying to jack an iPod?" She shook her head and talked around a mouthful of rice. "That's way harsh."

"My dad almost slapped me across the face last week," I said. I stared at the movie and shoveled food into my mouth.

Em's chopsticks froze mid-bite. "Your dad hit you?"

"No, but he had his hand raised. And the reason he didn't come tonight is that he was too drunk. He's been drinking a lot."

"You can't stay there anymore. Let's talk to Earl. Maybe that's abuse or neglect or something."

"One non-slap won't get me out of the house."

"What will you do if he does hit you?"

"I don't know. I do know that if either one of them ever hits Chrissy, neither of them will walk away."

There was a car I didn't recognize parked in the drive when Em's mom pulled in and a FOR SALE sign was in the yard. I guess Mom had been too busy getting her nest egg together to bother about me.

Mom gave me a quick glance and nothing else when I came in. She and a small man with a quick, birdlike manner pointed at an open ledger in his left hand. I headed up the stairs and ducked into Chrissy's room.

"Ames!" Chrissy attached herself to my legs. "Where've you been? Mom won't tell me. Everybody's been screaming and a man is here to take our furniture. I don't understand." Chrissy clutched me harder, her eyes watery and confused. "Will he take my bears?"

I picked her up and sat her in my lap on the bed. "I'm sure the man doesn't want your bears, but if he does, I'll fight him. He'll get two black eyes and a crunched-up nose if he touches one of your bears."

"He'd look funny," Chrissy said.

"He'd yell, 'Owie, owie, owie,'" I said.

Chrissy giggled. "That's what I used to say when I got hurt."

"That's right." I hugged her. "When he leaves, I'll talk to Mom and see what's up. Where's Dad?"

"He won't come out of his study. That's what all the screaming is. He told Mom he's on a roll."

Dad didn't come out of his study for two days. Our antique furniture was gone along with the silver, china, and crystal, and the two big chandeliers. I'd give odds that Mom's good jewelry was missing, too.

The realtor called that morning and Mom returned to the breakfast table. "You took out a second mortgage on the house? You forged my name?"

Dad's face was blank and gray.

"Not even the money I've got in the bank for all the

things I've sold will cover that. We can't get our equity out of this house."

Dad put his elbows on the table. Face in his hands. "You don't have any money in the bank."

Mom couldn't wrap her mind around what she just heard. "What did you say?" She looked here and there as if trying to place where she had mislaid something.

Dad moved his hands from his face but didn't look up. "I've been gambling online. I was up, really up, but the cards turned on me. When you put all that money in the account, I kept playing, trying to win back what I lost, but..."

"All that money is gone?" Mom's voice trembled, fading to a whisper. "You gambled it away?" Her eyes were wide in a thousand-yard stare. Like someone had smacked her across the forehead with a board and none of the synapses were firing.

"The money I took from the business was more than I told you," Dad stated, almost robotic. "My retirement wasn't enough. I had to get the second mortgage to cover it."

Dad hadn't just thrown Robin out on the street. He'd done it to us. Why hadn't it occurred to me that if he could do that to Robin, that he would do it to his wife and children? Why had I trusted anything he said at all? My stomach rolled over.

Mom grabbed the back of a chair, unsteady. She still had the stare and couldn't speak above a whisper. In short bursts. Disjointed in cadence. "We'll lose the house. *We won't have a house.* We won't have enough money to rent an apartment. We have one car and our clothes—" She stopped.

I thought Mom would faint. She sank into the chair. "What. Have. You. Done?"

IT'S OVER, BOULDER

Mom barged into my room without knocking and marched straight to my closets. "We're having a garage sale," she announced. I was still fighting nausea. I had heard Mom screaming—full-on banshee wailing—at Dad for a good while, then I couldn't hear anything. The study door slammed shut and mine flung open soon after. Mom was in fight mode.

First she pulled out all my school uniforms, then she found my heavy sweaters and stacked them on the bed. "Take anything you haven't worn in the last year, fold it, and add it to this stuff. We need money for a U-Haul trailer and the gas to get us to Texas." Was she in fight mode or flight mode?

"*Texas?*" I demanded, following her into the hall as she went into Chrissy's room.

"We won't have much room, so not much goes. I suggest you select wisely."

"This subdivision doesn't allow garage sales," I said.

"We won't be living here by the time they have a meeting of the committee. Let them sue me," Mom said. "Cheer up. You don't have to go back to school until we get settled."

"Why Texas?"

"Ask your father," Mom said.

I hurtled down the stairs and into the study.

"Why are we moving to Texas?" I burst out.

Dad slouched in the leather wingback chair, staring vacantly. Whatever the yelling had been about, he had been soundly defeated. "Your grandparents live there."

No. I don't have grandparents in Texas. I only have

one grandparent. No one, no one would lie to their own children about their grandparents.

"My..." I whispered, "My...your parents...are dead. You said...that's what...you said—"

Dad held up one hand to stop me. "Trust me, it's easier to say they are dead than to tell you the truth."

Trust him? I took a breath. "What truth?"

"They're penny-pinching monsters whose hearts shriveled up so long ago they can't remember having them."

I waited.

Dad looked at me. Saw I wanted more. "They're slumlords in a horrible, hard-scrabble town, and until now, I hadn't spoken to them since I went to college." He pushed out a breath. "Satisfied?"

If he could walk away from his own parents, when would he leave us?

"Then why are we going there?"

"Your mother said I've humiliated the family too much to live in Boulder anymore. Not that we can afford it." He looked down at the hardwood floor. When he pulled his head back up and gazed out the window, I saw the tears on his cheek. "She made me call them and ask if we could live in one of their rentals. I think this is her way of making sure I get a good dose of humiliation, too. I'm thinking prison might have been better."

He brushed the tear away. "Don't look at me like I'm full of self-pity. The only reason those two old wretches are letting us stay is because one of the rentals is so broken down it hasn't rented for six months. I have to fix the damn thing to get three free months' rent. And they'll get their pound of flesh out of me while I'm there."

I felt a warm flush of anger. "So on top of all the rest I've learned about you, I find out that you've lied to me my whole life about my grandparents?" I was practically breathless with indignation. "You're a gambler, a thief, *and* a hypocrite?" I counted on my fingers and stuck a fourth one out. "Oh, I forgot—add forgery to the list of crimes."

"I've already heard this speech from your mother." He ground the heels of his hands into his eye sockets.

Contempt now replaced the empty place I'd held for Dad. "I thought family was supposed to be what the Fords are all about."

"Mea culpa. Mea maxima culpa. I'm a pile of manure, and your and your mother's shit smells like roses."

Speechless. Dad had never talked to me like that before.

He cleared his throat and tried to redirect. "We'll be near Houston, and there're some good jobs there. Executive positions. People won't know me or my past.... And the cost of living is a lot better in Texas. It will be a good move. A fresh start."

HUMILIATION

I was left with two suitcases of clothes. A box of treasured pictures and mementos. My makeup, a couple of books, a camera, my pillows, and, after a fight, my laptop.

I watched strangers and, worse, neighbors and friends rummage through my CDs and clothes, our furniture, sheets, table linens, Dad's golf clubs, our bikes, tennis racquets, everything that made us *The Fords*. I died of shame when Mom forced me to make change.

I made a deal with Em to come and buy all of Chrissy's bears.

"That's kind of you, Emily, but there's no room in the car or the U-Haul for even one more box," Mom said.

"I'm going to mail them to her, Mrs. Ford." Em didn't even try to make nice.

Mom's face blazed with color. "Fine, then." She wouldn't make eye contact as she took Em's money, but her long look at me could have incinerated paper.

I walked out with Em. "Thanks for this, Em."

"How bad would it be to kidnap just one bear from a six-year-old? This one is really cute. Will Chrissy notice?"

She grinned at me. I couldn't help but grin back. "Chrissy would notice." We said it together. Nothing got past Chrissy.

I turned and trudged back to the garage to find Kim Banks, Layla Emerson, and Reggie Wilcox sashaying among the tables of our possessions.

Nightmare. I knew my friends didn't garage sale shop. Kim pointed at things but didn't touch, as if the objects were infectious. I guess sometimes a slap in the face isn't physical.

"There she is." Kim was loud, pulling the attention of

everyone in the garage. "Ames, you poor thing."

I tried to make my face a mask and tamp down the nausea that roiled in my stomach, but I couldn't control the blush that revealed my shame.

"There's a rumor that you're moving," Reggie said. "You know, the sign in front of your house and all, but you haven't said a word to anyone."

Layla made a sound like a cat coughing up a hair ball. "Like someone is going to buy your old school uniforms? How desperate is that? And CDs? Like everyone doesn't download." She put one manicured hand over her mouth. "Sorry, I didn't mean to say that. Really, good luck with the sale. My dad said the creditors are totally hounding you guys and...oh, I totally didn't mean to say that, either."

"Go away," I said. "And I totally meant to say that."

I turned and shot my mother a scathing look, then rushed into the house, searching for the nearest bathroom.

After the bits and pieces of our lives were carted off by strangers and pitying neighbors, Mom, Chrissy, and I cleaned the remains. Mom made a run and sold what was left to a secondhand store. Dad was in the kitchen, sitting on the floor drinking beer. I could have paid for Chrissy's bears myself with the money for that beer. He gambled away the big money and now he was drinking away the change. He looked more than pathetic, droopy-eyed and loose-limbed, propped into a corner.

Chrissy and I clattered across the rugless wood floors and up the stairs to her room.

"Everything echoes," Chrissy noticed.

"There's nothing to hear us, so our words just come back," I said. We flopped down on her plush carpet.

"Do you think Em will kidnap any of the bears?" I asked.

"Em's too nice," Chrissy said.

I laughed. "Those three words have never been spoken together in the history of mankind," I said.

Chrissy shook her head fiercely. "Em is nice, deep down. Sometimes she's nicer than you."

I felt like she'd just kicked me in the stomach. "What do you know?" I grumped. "You talk to stuffed bears."

*   *   *

"You're too drunk to drive, but I think you can manage to get the last of the suitcases into the back of the car," Mom shouted down the stairs to Dad, and then came into Chrissy's room. "Well, it's all done. Let's get in the car and go."

"I thought we were leaving in the morning," I said. "Em's coming by."

"Why sleep on these hard floors when we could be driving? Saying good-bye will just make you cry and give yourself a headache. Let's cut our losses and get going."

I wanted to argue with Mom for taking away my last thing of value: a good-bye with my best friend.

But she was already whipping down the hall.

Dad bumbled and fumbled with the suitcases. He arranged the already rearranged bags with Mom tapping her foot and snapping glances at her watch like we were about to miss a flight or something. Finally, she said, "Stop it. You're driving me insane. The suitcases are fine. They were fine ten minutes ago. Let's just go!"

That's when a '60s Volkswagen, hand-painted camouflage and purring like a cream-fed cat, drove up and angled across the nose of our Lexus SUV. Dad gave a big sigh of relief. Out of the passenger seat popped Rockin' Robin.

"Seconds from a clean getaway, were you?" Robin said.

"You called her?" Mom asked Dad.

"If you won't give me a hug good-bye, I'll take it by force," Robin said. She reached out and grabbed Mom in a fierce, hard hug. Mom seemed to crumple like an empty bag.

"At least this time I won't have to live in a tent." Mom tried to laugh but sobs came instead. She sank to the curb.

Robin sat next to her. "I'm moving in with Gretchen for a while. Randal has my phone number. I got a part-time job at a no-kill pet shelter. I just might get a hanker-ing to pet me a cow or two and come to Texas sometime. You never know with me."

"You never know. That's God's truth." Mom wiped her eyes. "I've lost everything important and you're blath-ering about petting cows."

Robin stood up slow and steady. She stepped away from Mom. "Last time I looked, your children were some-thing important, Diana."

She leaned into the car and kissed Chrissy. "I love you, dumpling. I'll call soon." I hugged her. "Take care of them," Robin whispered in my ear. "I love you."

She hugged Dad. "Thanks for calling. Now straighten up, asshole."

When Dad and I got into the car, Mom was already in the driver's seat with the motor running. She backed up, to avoid killing Robin's friend who still leaned against her camo Bug, then changed gears and drove away without another look at her mother.

Once on the interstate, Mom gripped the leather-covered steering wheel like her hands were fused into the ten and two position. Her seat was full upright and she never set the cruise control. No radio, no talking. She stared straight ahead, but there were sight daggers for Dad. He sighed and tilted his seat practically into my lap and went to sleep.

It got dark and the passing lights hypnotized me. I couldn't stretch out much with Dad's seat tilted back and Chrissy's booster seat anchored next to me. My legs were cramped and my back needed some stretching, but Mom made it clear that wouldn't happen any time soon.

"We're only stopping for gas and to pee. There's snacks and water. We don't have the cash for hotels or restaurants."

I decided drinking water would complicate matters. I dozed off for a while.

I woke up when Mom pulled in for gas. Dad sobered up enough to drive part of the way, so Mom took a nap. We all bailed to hit the bathrooms.

"It's official. Nothing is more disgusting than a gas station restroom," I snarked. But I had a surprise waiting for me in Texas—and a lesson about tempting the gods.

Once we got to our "destination," I begged Mom to let us live in the car. Any little hope of a life I recognized vanished when we turned onto Poverty Lane, as I called it.

The houses were crowded one next to another with scraggly yards, bare patches of dirt surrounded by unmowed grass that crawled up chain-link fences. Pit bulls and rottweilers strained against their chains as we drove by. Porches and roof lines sagged, curtains hung haphazardly, parting to let suspicious faces watch us covertly. Of all the run-down, pathetic houses, we turned into the carport of the worst.

Peeled and blistered paint made the house look like it had leprosy, front window broken, door hanging agape like a first grader's dangling front tooth, bits of shingle missing from the roof, and wild overgrown grass. Its only saving grace was a tangle of briars along one side where, almost in defiance, roses bloomed. Not many. Just enough soft beauty to highlight the raw ugliness. Home sweet home.

"Let's go look at the damage before we unload," Dad said.

Opening the car door was nearly a fatal mistake. Early April in Boulder is still cold. We left in sweaters and jeans. We stepped out into a sauna. Swamp-monster humid. Clammy pop-sweat-out-on-your-forehead-in-seconds hot. I was skinning off my sweater quicker than I could draw another labored breath. Geez, you could eat this air easier than breathe it.

I wiped my face with the sleeve of the sweater and then pulled the tail of my T-shirt out of my jeans and flapped it. "We cannot live here," I moaned.

"Maybe it's not as bad inside," Dad said.

He was so wrong. It had been used as a drug flop-house or something until it got too gross for skuzzballs. Hypodermic needles littered the floor, as did human feces and animal crap. Pizza boxes and Chinese takeout settled in corners and heaped in piles in every room. Newspaper bits that had been used for toilet paper littered the bathroom floor. A dead rat floated in the toilet bowl.

I walked out and got back in the car. Mom and Dad followed.

Mom took a deep breath. "Here's the plan," she began, summoning her inner organizer to help her cope, I guess. "I can't face cleaning that up without sleep. Randal, we'll go to your parents' — your mother and father will just have to deal. We'll have a nap, then buy supplies and do a major clean and disinfect. The girls and I do that while you fix the door and window. We can sleep on the floors once they are clean and move our stuff in tomorrow."

I made a loud blatting noise, like the sound of the buzzer in a game show. "Wrong. I'm never stepping foot in that place again. Kill me if you want. Put me up for adoption. Leave me on a street corner with hookers and drug addicts and let me find my way back to Boulder. But I'm done with Texas. Officially over."

Mom didn't even turn around. "Tell someone who cares."

Part 2

Part 2

THE GENE
POOL IS POISON

My grandparents' house was in a neighborhood of geezers. Their houses were geezered, too. Painted mailboxes with ducks or flowers on it, concrete statuary in the yards with cheap flowers around the bases. Cherubs, angels, saints, or worse, gnomes. The place was an ode to bad taste.

Dad's geezers acted like the British army had arrived to bivouac in their house when we arrived. No smiles, no welcoming hugs. They stared at us like the strangers we were and at Dad like...well, like they didn't trust him. They ushered us in with worried looks. Had we already caught leprosy from that house?

Chrissy stepped up. "Do I call you Grandmom like our grandmom Robin or what?"

The old woman stepped back, glaring at Dad. "Well, since I've never set eyes on you 'til this minute, I think Mrs. Ford will do right fine, little miss." I ground my teeth.

So, we couldn't look forward to a love fest here. I couldn't blame them. How cold could Mom and Dad be? To not even tell these people that they had grandchildren? But when Dad hit bottom he called for a handout. Couldn't we have gone on welfare or something in Colorado?

"Ma," Dad said, "we drove straight through. You have to know what that house looks like. We just need to sleep a few hours before we can get to work. We're not here to steal your paintings."

Dad shrugged toward a wall. Hanging there in a dime store frame was a magazine picture of JFK. Seriously.

"Wouldn't be the first time you stole from us," Dad's mother said. "I'll get you something to drink. You looked parched."

Mom's head snapped around to Dad in surprise. I could see in her expression that those words were clattering around in her head like they were in mine.

Wouldn't be the first time you stole from us.

Dad's mother brought us warm tap water to drink from plastic cups. The floors in the house were vomit green linoleum, the furniture was Goodwill rejects, and their clothes were Kmart Blue Light Specials. Fine, I'm a snob. I was tired, sweaty, road-gritty, and all I wanted to do was bawl my head off, but I wouldn't give my parents the satisfaction of seeing me break.

"Where's my bedroom?" I asked.

"Well, now, she's something," Mrs. Ford said. "There's no 'your' bedroom. Why would there be one when I haven't even heard a howdy from you ever?"

I didn't know how to politely explain to someone that they were supposed to be worm food.

"There's a single bed in the room Doreen uses for

sewing. Y'all can fight for that and the others can bed down on the floor." This from Mr. Ford. "Hope you got your own pillows and quilts for the floor." He hitched his sagging trousers and shuffled out of the room.

Mom and Chrissy doubled up on the twin bed. Dad tossed his pillow on the bare linoleum and lay down. He didn't even take off his shoes. I stretched out on a braided rug that smelled slightly of dog.

Against all odds, I slept, only to be awakened by Mr. Ford. "Y'all need to get up. It's dinner time and Doreen's got chili."

They were going to feed us? I could do chili. I got up and stretched. I felt like someone had been walking on me with heavy boots. I peeled my sweat-dampened T-shirt away from my body and shook it, once again trying for a little cooling air. How could it be this hot?

When we assembled at the table Mrs. Ford served the bowls of rice and chili. The chili was made of beans in a watery but spicy sauce. The beverage? The tepid tap water again. No ice.

"Are you vegetarians?" I asked.

"We live on a fixed income," Mrs. Ford snapped at me. "We can only afford meat twice a week. There's plenty of protein in beans."

"It's good," I muttered. "Some of my friends are vegetarians, that's all."

"Do you all know what your father done to us the last time we seen him?" Mrs. Ford asked, her chin low to her chili bowl and her eyes narrowed into slits.

Dad put down his spoon and launched into a protest before they even had a chance to explain. "You owed me that money. I'd been picking up rent checks every month for two years. It wasn't easy. You never paid me a cent for it."

"We fed you and clothed you and gave you a roof," said Mr. Ford.

Mom's expression told me that she had heard a different version of this story. "Randal?" She was demanding an explanation.

"I got accepted to University of Texas." Dad's voice was curt and defensive. "I managed to scrape together the deposit fees but didn't have the money for the first semester.

So I collected the checks and I took the bus to Austin."

"You stole from your own kin," Dad's mother insisted.

"Hardly," Dad retorted. "Everything I owned fit in a backpack."

His father grunted his contempt. "Only reason we let you come back is we wanted to see you crawl."

So...Dad's stealing wasn't a one-time desperate act. But look at what he had lived with. I didn't know how to feel. The chili disagreed with me.

We finished in silence. Not even Chrissy knew what to say.

After grabbing our pillows, we hauled to a Home Depot for industrial-strength cleaner/disinfectant and an assortment of other cleaning supplies. We were going to do battle. I didn't give us a chance of winning. That house needed a blowtorch, not Lysol and a few trash bags.

When Dad turned off the motor at Brokedown Palace, Mom turned on him. "You told me your parents abused you emotionally and used you as free labor. You didn't mention you stole from them."

Dad said nothing.

"I might have understood. That wasn't enough. You had to make yourself a hero. You never worked for a year waiting tables and saving tips and eating leftovers from the restaurant to get your first semester's fees. What a sob story. You're pathetic."

For the first time, I agreed with Mom. I didn't know my own father. All the times he had been WonderDad, it hadn't been to please us. It had been to make him look good.

"I need a beer," Dad muttered.

Mom sorted through our purchases. She handed Dad rubber gloves, a couple of trash bags, and a dustpan. "The rat, the syringes, and the piles of shit are yours. When you're done with those, the girls and I will come in and start cleaning."

Dad sighed, but he took the stuff without a word.

Chrissy broke the silence. "I don't want to clean," she whined. "I'm too little."

"Too bad," I said. "If I have to clean, you do, too."

"You don't have to clean, Chrissy," Mom said. "You

are too little. You can bring me the broom or the mop or a trash bag when I need it. How's that?"

Terrific. I officially hated everyone.

While Dad was in the house, a car drove up and parked, three boys tumbled out dressed in old shorts, ragged tees, and sneakers. Two stood to one side, while one reached into the car and pulled out a box, checked the label, and strode toward our car.

"Excuse me, would one of you be Chrissy Ford?"

Chrissy's head lowered and she slid her eyes for a sideways look. She was waiting for something bad to happen. I knew the feeling.

"My name is Thomas Caldwell. I think you might know Emily Keifer?" He balanced the box on one jutted hip and scratched behind his ear with his other hand.

"My bears!" Chrissy squealed right in my ear. Deaf in one ear might not be so bad if it meant that I would only hear half the crap I'd been hearing.

Chrissy bailed out of the car and practically ran up Thomas Caldwell like a squirrel runs up an oak. He put the box on the curb and Chrissy ripped the tape.

"Em's my best friend," I told the guy.

"Hi, you must be Ames," he said. "Em and I know each other from Facebook. When she found out you were moving to Texas she sent out an SOS to see if anyone lived near Foley. None of her friends did, but one of her friends is a friend of mine, and, well, you know how that works."

I did.

"My friend Brad hooked me up with Em—wirelessly, not, you know, biblically—and she told me you'd be needing a friend and that she wanted special care delivery for this package. She also told me that your house was going to need some work. I drove by a couple of days ago. It's going to need more than 'some' work, I think. So, Ames, Mrs. Ford, if you don't mind, I lassoed some friends to welcome you to Texas and help out a little."

Oh, kill me now. Em had paid these guys to help us shovel our hovel.

He pointed back to the boys standing by his car. They now held rakes, shovels, and heavy lawn bags. "Those aren't for landscaping. I walked through the inside. I didn't think brooms or mops should touch the first few layers. Of course, you'll be the boss. In the South, women always are. Southern men are smart enough to understand and accept that."

Mom smiled. Smiled. Had she lost her mind? She was falling for this chicken-fried bullshit.

Tom introduced Devon and Marc. Marc didn't look exactly thrilled to be here, but he did give me a half smile that seemed to communicate he knew that I wasn't thrilled to be here, either. That singled him out as the one least likely to be the boy scout. The one Dad would like the least. The one Mom didn't smile at. That made him interesting. He wasn't an obvious hungry-like-a-wolf bad boy, but he was not a cute, big-eyed pup either. He was the one I wanted to know.

Dad came out with a bag and plopped it on the curb. The introductions and explanations made the rounds again. "Em has her networks, doesn't she?"

Mom turned to Chrissy, who was counting and studying her bears. "Sweetie, there's no reason for you to step inside this filthy house now that we have more helpers.

Stay in the shade of this big oak and play with your bears. I can see you from the windows and door. Okay?" Mom retrieved a blanket for the little princess and Chrissy moved her bears to her new, clean castle with the fresh outdoor scent.

Mom handed me rubber gloves and disinfectant. "While the boys do the floors, you can take care of the kitchen counters. I'm getting rid of all those filthy curtains and washing the windows."

I went in to survey the damage. Rotten food. Pizza boxes squirming with maggots, liquids turned to stone on the countertops and the sink, a cesspool of things I didn't want to imagine. While the worst she got was window grime she would clean with Windex and paper towels? Thanks, Mom. I wanted to chew stones and spit gravel at her.

While I stared at the mess, Marc came over. "Here, use this." He handed me a scraperlike thing with a wide blade, then inserted one black lawn bag into another. "Double bag, always double bag. You don't want a leak and any of that stuff splashing on your skin."

He crinkled his nose in disgust at the mess and made a wry bit of a smile. It was a little lopsided because one tooth kind of lapped over another just the tiniest bit. It made me want to ruffle his shaggy hair.

"Do *not* touch anything with your bare hands. Shove everything with this scraper into the bags. Scrape until the counter is clean, then call me to help with that sink. Okay?"

I didn't answer.

"Promise?" he urged.

"Scout's honor," I said, and set to work. I glanced back and he was still looking at me. I blushed and he grinned. He tilted his head almost imperceptibly and raised his eyebrows. "Busted," he whispered.

Marc went back to the dutiful duo and their raking and shoveling. The guys made quick work and had moved on to industrial brooms to shove the smaller stuff into piles, then used a regular broom to push that stuff into bags. Marc pulled off a silver piece of duct tape and wrapped it around the broom handle. "That's the contaminated broom. Best not to use it on clean floors."

Dad leaned on the industrial broom. "You really know how to do this right. Have you cleaned out old houses before?"

Marc hesitated, then shrugged. "We live in one of your parents' houses. That's why Tom thought of me to come help. Ours wasn't this bad, but it did need work."

"Are you handy with a hammer and nails and paintbrushes?"

"Yup, done it all. Can even replace that windowpane."

"Looking for a little after school work?"

"I'm home-schooled. My schedule is pretty flexible," Marc said.

"Home-schooled?"

Devon butted in. "His dad is a Fundamentalist. He thinks the high school is a den of evil or a bed of inequity."

"That's a den of iniquity, moron." Marc sighed. "Most of my church is home-schooled, sir. It's just the way my dad wants it."

"Nothing wrong with keeping temptation out of your path," Dad said.

Well, that's the only way Dad would avoid it. I needed to watch this more. I think Dad was seeing a lot of himself in Marc. Smart, capable, from crappy circumstances. He liked him. Then again, he saw a lot of himself in Marc, and look how he turned out. Five-minute psychology is essentially useless, but first impressions...like I said. I wanted to watch this more. Marc was certainly watchable.

Marc turned to me. "Ready for the sink?"

"Nobody's ready for that sink."

He got a bucket and what looked like a thing you use to scoop fish from an aquarium. "Stand back, I'm going in."

He dunked the net into the murky water and scooped out a clog. The water drained.

"My advice is to pour Clorox in there and spray it down before you touch anything. Even if you have rubber gloves. I'll put this"—he indicated the mess in the net—"in the barrel that goes to the dump. Don't touch any part of yourself with those gloves. Okay?"

I smiled. "Got it." I almost saluted, but that would mean touching my forehead. Marc was cool. He acted like he honestly cared if I lived or died. Mom and Dad had given me the nastiest job in the house. Chrissy was outside so she didn't even have to sniff a few fumes. Mom was washing windows with the other two boys after they shoveled the floors. She was laughing and practically flirting with them.

I considered this odd trio of males as I uncapped the Clorox. They had separated into the two and one dynamic immediately. They knew Marc, but I'd bet money they didn't roll with him. They were all dressed like vagrants, but the teeth and hair gave it away. Tom and Declan/Duncan/whatever-his-name-was were orthodontic perfection. Nature didn't make teeth that straight or that shade of white. My parents had the old bills from our dentist to prove it. The dentally delightful duo with the lazy swagger/shoulder rolls also had short, expensive hairstyles.

Marc's hair was longer and rumpled. Stoner hair. Bangs down to his brows. The overlap on his front teeth that made him look like an appealing first grader but cut him from the high roller herd. Home-schooled? Fundamentalist? Lives in this neighborhood? He was kind of a mystery. I liked that.

Marc came back in, checked my progress, and looked through his bag of tricks. He returned with another kind of plastic scraper that made quick work of the dried gunk that my scraper or the sponge were no match for. "You're so good at this, you kind of scare me. A little too Becky Home-Ec-y, you know."

"I had a good teacher," I said.

His smile was slow, soft. "You're just all brand-new, aren't you?" He winked at me. "You don't belong here." He jutted his chin, indicating the house. "The other guys came because your friend—"

"Paid them," I said.

"She got totally unobtainable concert tickets. The girl must be connected. These guys totally agree that you are smokin' hot but think you're too young—"

"That means 'flat-chested.' Excuse me, I have to go somewhere and die of embarrassment."

Marc smiled the lopsided smile. "Let me finish. Like I said, I think you're brand-new. None of that 'oh my god!' and 'is this fingernail polish to die for?' stuff."

"No, I'm not that girl," I said.

"You and your parents—you, especially—don't fit here. I know how that is. Not to fit."

"Yeah," I said. "I don't fit because I keep getting tossed out of the boat." I shot a poison-arrow glance at my mother.

Marc's face softened. His bottom lip did this little twitch thing that made him, I don't know, look like a child lost in a crowded mall. So vulnerable.

"Tossed out of the boat. That's a great way to put it." He turned to scrub the other side of the sink so our conversation would become inconspicuous. "Yeah, I'm familiar with the feeling. It's how I knew."

"Knew what?" I whispered the words, but it didn't matter because the rest of the world had fallen away. There was a cocoon wrapped around Marc and me. His eyes were gentle and understanding.

"I know your family betrayed you."

I gasped, and a tear leaked out from my left eye.

"I'd wipe that away, but my hands are wet and *they* would see. You need to wipe it off. Don't ever let them see that you have a soft place."

I hunched my shoulder and wiped my cheek against it. I wasn't stupid. I knew he had just divided the group into "them" and "us," but he had seen into me. The other two bozos were over there flashing their teeth to my mom.

I regained composure and scraped the counter. "Do you always psychoanalyze everyone you meet?" The sentence was clipped and a little cold.

"Nope. I know the signs because I've been through it. I see how you protect yourself when you talk to them. Me, I started collecting…" He paused, leaned in, and whispered, "Guns."

Guns?

I froze in mid-scrub. Something in his tone told me he wasn't talking about hunting rifles. Deer, elk, squirrel. Why be so secretive about that? I *was* in Texas… I looked around me to see if we had caught anyone's attention. No.

His voice dropped and he moved even closer to my ear. "Does that scare you?" His voice dropped even lower. "I can protect you if you want."

I pulled back and stared at him. I don't know what my expression was. Something in his voice or the way he watched my face told me I was being tested. I was chilled, but I was on fire. At the same time. My heart raced, but my breathing stopped. All of me was still.

This was...strange.

Marc knew what he was doing. He was cutting me off from the herd. He was telling me he had secrets. Dark ones. He knew I'd be either repulsed and afraid—or fascinated. Seeing an offer of shared power. I could accept him or reject him now.

We locked eyes and made an unspoken promise. I wasn't going to tell about his guns, and he...he was going to be on my side.

It happened that quickly. I was hot and tired and sore and pissed off. I had been the good girl and gotten a lap full of betrayal. I wanted to be dangerous, and danger winked and told me I could.

I accepted.

After we'd shoveled, swept, re-swept, vacuumed, de-cobwebbed, mopped, and disinfected, I was ready to be hospitalized. Tom and the other shoveler, Kevin or Delwin or whatever, decided they had done their cheerful duty and bailed. Marc, however, told Dad that if he wanted to put some plastic over the window and board over the door for the night, he'd help do that in exchange for a ride home.

While they hammered and boarded and sealed, we brought in sleeping bags, pillows, changes of clothes, and toiletries, and then Mom—using the only cell phone, of which she had total and unrelinquished control—ordered pizza. She insisted Marc stay. A mantra ran through my head. *Guns, Mom. Mad Marc.* I had to hold back a bit, make my parents think I wasn't interested so they would push me right toward what they would hate most.

Em would love this.

"Marc," Mom said, "it's got to be eighty degrees. Is this normal for spring?"

"April is a good month. Early in the month it's always between seventy-five and eighty-five degrees. It'll have some ninety-plus days by the end of April. May will jump around in the high eighties and low nineties, and all of July and August run high nineties and up into the hundreds."

Chrissy didn't react because she didn't understand what that meant. The rest of us did. If it was this hot and it was only eighty degrees...

"Randal, didn't you tell me that there's no air-conditioning?"

Dad didn't answer.

"We will all *die*," I said. I turned to Marc. "Will we roast from the outside, like in an oven, or inside out like a microwave?"

He didn't lose a beat. "Neither. You'll sweat into a puddle like the Wicked Witch of the West."

Dad didn't laugh. He guffawed. Seriously. That was the sound. Then he started talking to Marc about how often and when he could work. Blah, blah. Chrissy focused on eating the cheese strings that trailed from her pizza slice. I ate mine like a zombie, still calculating heat and no air-conditioning.

"Ames, can you clean this up when everyone's done?" Mom called out to me. She smiled and looked at me, then at Marc. "I'm done in. I'm taking a shower and climbing into the sleeping bag."

"Let me help you with that," Marc said to me. Okay, now I got it. Mom was setting us up. Not so quick, Mommy Dearest.

"Nah, I can handle a couple of boxes and soda cans. Dad, don't you need to run Marc home? I'm sure he's beat."

Marc jerked his head toward me and his jaw hardened. I looked down, then sort of up through my lashes at him like I'd seen Em do a million times. The set of his mouth relaxed as he snapped to the game.

I turned my back on Marc and gathered the trash. Dad groaned as he hoisted himself from the floor.

Mom and Dad, you're about to find out how much betrayal hurts.

LEARNING TO ADJUST

I woke up in my new bedroom with paralysis. Parts of me could move, but it hurt so bad that I didn't want to risk it after the first effort. My arms and shoulders were like one large bruise that someone was knuckling. I had no idea how many times I had squatted yesterday, but my butt and my quads were announcing that it had been too many.

I was on my back and the view of the mildew on the ceiling wasn't helping my mood. I didn't think I could turn my head, so I slid my eyes as far to the right as I could. There was Chrissy, snoring like a little cat purrs, dewed with sweat, sprawled on top of her sleeping bag, surrounded by her bears. If she woke up smiling and chirping as she usually did, I would be forced to drown her. *No way,* I thought. *In my condition, she could take me easily.*

I heard groaning from the other room. Mom and Dad had awakened to hit the same hard wall I had. Dad let out a string of curse words that would curl a preacher's hair and that a sailor would admire. Mom didn't bother to admonish him.

There were more groans then more shuffling. Three raps on our door and it swung open. Dad looked like he slept in the washer on the spin cycle. "I don't know what's worse—the heat or the pain. You sore?"

"I'm paralyzed. I think there was some hideous new germ in all that gunk I touched." I whimpered. "I have a fever and I'm dying."

"Die later. You have to paint today." He shambled away.

I repeated Dad's earlier string of curse words in my head and directed them his way. Wasn't this child abuse?

Slavery? Something I could call the authorities about?

I lurched to my feet and headed straight for the shower, hoping hot water would ease my misery. No deal. Mom was in the one bathroom. Steam billowing out over the plastic shower curtain.

"Save some hot water for someone else," I shouted.

Mom stuck her head from around the curtain. "What?"

"There's only a thirty-gallon tank. I know because you and Dad used it all up last night and I had to shower in cold water."

"Just let me rinse out my hair."

It was too late. The steam was gone and Mom shrieked when the hot water turned cold on her head.

Crap. I had no idea how long it would take for that thing to reheat. I went back to bed.

Mom came in wearing shorts and a tee. "Your dad has gone to Home Depot to get stuff for the door and paint and brushes."

"I'm too thrilled," I snarked.

"Since I know you're cranky about the shower and that's my fault, I'll let that slide. But Ames, if we are going to make it through all"—she shrugged and waved her hands in the air helplessly—"*this*, you have to lose the lousy attitude. It's bad enough without listening to your constant whining."

Fine, I won't whine. I won't say anything to her, then.

"Now, get up and let's get to work."

I stayed put.

Chrissy piped up. I had no idea she'd been awake. "If Daddy isn't here with paint and brushes, how is there any work yet?"

Finally, the voice of reason.

"Your sister and I have to wipe down all the walls and ceilings with bleach to kill the mold and mildew. If we don't, it'll come right back through the new paint."

What was that new and colorful word Dad had used this morning? *Shitfoot.* I think it was the feeling you got when you'd just stepped in it.

"Chrissy, go outside and play. I know you'll be hot, but the bleach is bad for you to breathe," Mom said. "First there's juice and donuts. Dad got those last night on the way home from Marc's."

Mom turned to me. "Ames, you might be interested to know that Marc has offered to help on a regular basis. He doesn't have a job, his home-schooling keeps him flexible, and he says helping out will keep him from being bored. He wants no payment except meals when he's here. Awfully generous, don't you think?" Her expression was a mystery.

So Marc would be here today. That meant I'd have to suffer the cold shower so I could wash my hair. No makeup, though. That would look like I was trying. I had learned a lot at the Em Academy.

I wore a thick pair of yellow rubber gloves and swabbed the walls in long stripes when Marc and Dad strode in. Marc dropped his bags of tools on the floor and hurried over to me.

"Watch out. You're getting chemical burns." He guided me with a hand on my elbow like he was Ashley Wilkes and I was Miss Scarlett and put my hands under the tap. After washing the gloves he folded the tops back into a cuff. "Now when you lift up, the bleach will spill into the cuff and not run onto your arms."

I glanced around to see if Mom and Dad were watching this show of concern. Getting the idea that I might be valuable to someone. Nope. I guess they were in the bedroom or outside where the bleach fumes wouldn't hurt them.

Marc pulled my arms under the spigot and let the cold water run a long time, then gently rubbed soap on the already reddened places, then rinsed again. "Do you have some kind of, I don't know, what's the word for that greasy kind of medical stuff—not lotion. Oh, unguent? Is that it?"

"Yeah," I said. "The lotions and potions are about the only thing we unpacked besides the sleeping bags." And the towels. Mom couldn't release all her thick, luxurious towels.

"Show me." It was a gentle command. But it was a command, not a request. Why did my head go swimmy?

I took him to the bathroom and he spread the gooey stuff on my arms, holding my rubber-gloved hands and rolling my arms back and forth to find any red places that might be hiding from him.

"I thought about you all night," he said. "You shouldn't be doing this kind of work. Your parents could give you something else to do. I watched last night. They treat you like a servant."

How was I supposed to play hard to get when he was reading my mind?

"You should go fix my mom's gloves. She didn't make cuffs, either," I pointed out.

"She can take care of herself," Marc said. "I can take care of you." He stepped back, stared into my eyes, assessing. He studied my face. I think he found what he was looking for, because his mouth relaxed into a half smile. "I've got the...means."

"Huh?"

He leaned in close. His breath was warm against my cheek. "I've got a handgun on me."

My eyelashes fluttered against his cheek. Was this another test? Had I passed?

"It's okay, I have a concealed weapons permit."

"I thought you couldn't get one of those unless you were twenty-one," I whispered.

"I'm twenty-two. But I tell everyone I'm younger."

I leaned back to look at him. Now I was assessing. Yes,

he could be older. He wasn't lying. I felt sure he wasn't.

"I look young and when I try to hang with people my age, I get the shit beat out of me. In fact, that's why I started buying guns." His eyes still never left my face. Still watching, testing, evaluating.

Why would he tell me this? Why not? He said he had a permit. He was legal. If I backed away, he would know I wasn't the girl he wanted. If I said nothing…that dark thing thrummed in me. I heard its hum in my ears.

A rush of cold then hot took over me. My mouth filled as if I had just bitten into sweet fruit. My eyes locked on to his. "Where is it?" I whispered.

He grinned. "Ankle holster, covered by a heavy sock. Left. I'm left-handed."

"Can I touch?"

"Make it quick. Your parents are going to wonder what's going on in here."

I squatted and reached out for his left ankle. There it was. Compact and hard.

And the most insane part—it didn't scare me. It excited me like nothing ever had.

It flashed through my head that the gun thrilled me more than Marc did. Until now, I had no power. Now I had an ally. I had secrets. I could betray.

I wanted to howl like Em and I had when we were high. As I stood, I slid my hand up Marc's leg until it rested on his hip. My fingertips shook with my forwardness.

"That's..." I whispered.

"Yeah, I know what you mean. Nobody knows it but you, but you're the big dog on the front porch when you're carrying." My eyes widened. Not the dogs going crazy barking in the backyard, but the big dog on the front porch.

I didn't know Marc. I didn't know why he picked me. I didn't care. I had to have him. He knew me. He'd found me. I'd out-Em'd Em in the wild boy department. That dark that lived in me would slither from its cage. Would be unleashed. I would be new.

It took us most of the day to wipe down all the walls and ceilings. Marc brought me protective glasses and a hat when I stood on the ladder and swiped at the ceiling.

"You need to let the bleach dry completely. Overnight. Let this place air out, too. I think you guys should call it a day," Marc suggested. "I'll go get a bucket of chicken if you like and you can go to sleep early. We can get this whole place painted inside tomorrow if we push it."

"This hasn't been pushing it?" I asked.

"Sure. You've been pushing hardest of all. Your dad and I need to kick in a little harder. We've spent most of our time at Home Depot, while the real work has been going on here." He gave me a fake shoulder punch.

I wanted to crawl up his body. I wanted to drag him into the shower with me.

"Everybody outside. Breathe fresh air. I'll bring chicken and aspirin." He looked at Dad.

"You're a take-charge kind of kid, aren't you? I like that." He handed Marc some money. "I'm too old for this."

We followed Marc out. Mom and Dad sat on the porch step, and I stretched out under the tree with Chrissy.

"Am I in detention?"

"No, you're in heaven," I said. "I'm in hell."

"But we're not dead," Chrissy said.

"Speak for yourself," I told her. But the honest truth was that I was finally starting to feel alive again.

When Marc got back with the chicken, we had a picnic outside. Dad stretched out on his back, cradling his head in his laced fingers. "I'd forgotten how warm it got so soon. The summers are brutal."

Marc sat next to Dad, his forearms resting loosely on his bent knees. "None of these houses have duct work for central air. You're going to need a couple of window units—you know, air conditioners."

Dad sat up. "There's no money in the budget for those. Those things run up the electric bill like grease through a goose." Dad was reverting to Southern-speak in less than a day.

"Box fans, then. At least for the bedrooms. If you plan on sleeping, you need something to cancel out the street noise around here."

Marc had a point. It was a far cry from our quiet zone in Boulder, buffered by landscaping, purring cars, and people with insulated lives. This neighborhood was a carnival. People came and went all day, sat on porches and in yards. Souped-up junkers roared, loud music poured from boom boxes or out of open windows—hip-hop, rap, Tejano, and country all blending to a Babel-like cacophony. Loud voices arguing, shouting out their frustrations at living here, I supposed.

I tuned back in to Dad as he laid out the game plan. "Ames, you and Mom will paint the inside while Marc and I scrape the outside of the house."

Had he gone crazy? Or had the bleach fumes gotten to me and I was hearing things? If I heard what I thought, I didn't have to worry about Dad anymore—Mom would brain him with one of those paint cans.

"Um, Mr. Ford," Marc said. "I'm sorry to interrupt, but if all of us work on the inside painting, you'll be able to move your furniture inside. That way you'll be much more comfortable with your own belongings and your beds. You'll rest better, you know."

Dad pulled the straw back and forth through the plastic top of his Coke. The squeaking noise made my head feel like something inside it was leaking out of my ears. Someone was making an effort to take care of me, and it appeared Dad was deciding if I was worth the effort.

"That's a good idea, Marc. But we don't have beds and mattresses. We sold all that. The girls will have to share a room and that means twin beds, and Mrs. Ford and I are going to have to make do with a double in that postage-stamp room of ours."

He fiddled with his straw again. Couldn't he stop with the squeaking straw? The pressure in my head was going to make my eyes pop out and splat on the ground.

"Let's call it a day. We can't do much until the walls dry out from the bleach water. I'll go buy mattresses if Marc will take me." He looked at Mom. "You could take our car to buy sheets and rugs and order blinds. Don't forget the blinds have to be white like the walls."

Mom looked up. "I can handle that. I have the measurements. Just get the mattresses and box springs that have the screw-on legs so we don't have to buy bed frames."

"Hold it," I said. "I don't even get to pick the color for

my room?" I ached for the so-soft-you-almost-couldn't-tell-it-was-there lavender color of my old room.

"Nope," Dad said. "All the walls have to be white. Blinds have to be white. The outside is going to be white with beige trim, so it doesn't fade. That's how rental houses have to be. Pretty much no personality allowed."

"Okay..." I started thinking. No personality. A clean slate, right? "I want stuff that's all white, too. Sheets, bed-spread, rug, whatever you get, it has to be totally white." That would work. I was about to reinvent myself.

"Ames, get over yourself. I need to find what's on sale. I can't run all over looking for..." Mom stopped, but her anger kept rising. "You're in no position to be making custom orders anymore. None of us are. You can stay here and put the pots and pans and dishes in the cupboards. Hang clothes in the closets."

She may as well have said, *Breathe the poison air for a few more hours. Maybe that will put us out of our misery.*

I scowled at her, then glanced at Marc. He wasn't look-ing at Mom, but he was listening. He was pissed.

Mom showered, again, and had Chrissy in tow as she

came into the kitchen to get the keys. I was shelving coffee mugs, chucking them roughly into the cupboard, as Mom moved toward me. "Your attitude is certainly *not* appreciated here. Why don't you try actually being helpful, instead of being such an ungrateful little bitch?"

She had never called me a name like that. It stung more than I imagined possible.

Couldn't all this just stop? I didn't want to fight all the time. I was so tired.

"Mom." I turned to her. "Don't. Please don't be like this."

Mom shut her eyes and her shoulders slumped. I stepped forward and reached out to hug her.

"Don't!" It was that hard, angry whisper. "Take your share of the responsibility and get over yourself. I'm *sick* of carrying the rest of you on my shoulders." She snatched her keys and spun out of the kitchen.

After she left, I shook too hard to pick up the plates that I needed to put away. There was a place inside, a place that used to love Mom, that felt empty now.

Is that what love is, something that slinks away in the

night when everyone is busy looking out for themselves? Had we only loved each other when it was easy?

I was still unpacking kitchen items when Dad and Marc drove up with mattresses and box springs. "Let's leave them on the porch," Dad said.

Marc put one finger to his head, then pushed it up and down through his hair. A nervous tic I was to see often. "Um, I don't think that's a good idea...." He looked up and down the street.

"Oh," Dad said. "I keep forgetting where I am. Okay, in the living room with everything."

They lugged the stuff in and left the plastic wrapping on, but I stretched out on one of the twin sets anyway.

Dad popped open a can from a six-pack of beer. "You have brothers and sisters?" he asked Marc.

"Not here. They're still with my mom. I moved here when I got..." Marc stopped. He looked squarely at Dad. "I got to be a real handful when Mom and Dad divorced. I started running with a bad crowd. We all decided it would be best for me to come here and live with Dad. Be home-schooled, go to church with Dad, get away from my friends in California. Straighten myself out."

Dad nodded. "I certainly understand that. Trying to get a new start. In a new place." He chugged the rest of his beer and popped another.

Painting the inside of the house went fast with four of us working. Marc and I did my room first, then the bathroom and the kitchen. Mom and Dad did the hall, their room, and the living room. It was late when we finished and everyone was beat.

"I'm too tired to bring in the box springs for the beds. Let's just spread the mattresses out on the floor and sleep on them here," Dad said.

Marc slid a look to me. "I'm okay. Why don't you let me put Ames's and Chrissy's beds together?" He turned to Chrissy. "Hey, Bear Herder, you can help me put the sheets on, while Ames takes a shower. I'll bet you've been wanting to help."

Chrissy, bored from playing alone for days, was up like a shot and full of smiles.

"You are...beyond great," I told Marc. "I'm heading to the shower first, then I'll help."

When I trekked out of the shower, the ugly room had already been turned into a fairy tale. I saw a small white rug next to a twin bed pushed against the wall. The bed was made with white sheets and a single pillow, and a white bedspread draped down to the floor, hiding the metal legs of the box spring. A single pink rose rested against the pillow. I knew they bloomed outside the window of this room, but Marc had taken the trouble to leave a message.

A message. That he might be more to me than an avenue to power and danger? Someone who might give me the affection and care that I could no longer find?

"We had to work real fast on your bed so he could be gone before you came out," Chrissy said.

"Thanks—it's great," I said. Almost a whisper. Mom hired a decorator to do my room in Boulder, but it didn't make my head and heart race like this. I had been so naive then. I thought Mom had done all that to make me happy, but she had just thrown money at someone to have a showcase bedroom.

"Can you help me with my bed?"

I looked over. Marc had screwed the legs onto Chrissy's bed and set the mattress on the springs, but she was on the mattress falling onto her little butt trying to tug the fitted sheet into place.

"Wow, you went blue." Understatement. Everything was neon blue with yellow and purple flowers. A color riot in one corner and hospital sterile in the other. I picked Chrissy up and set her on the floor. As I made her bed I smiled. Mom and Dad had drained my world of color, but Marc was bringing it back. One little color at a time.

TRUTH OR DARE

The next morning, Marc drove up in his old truck and knocked politely on the door.

"Marc, it's Sunday. You can take a day off," Dad said, even though Marc was obviously not dressed to paint.

"Yes, sir. I meant to ask last night, but I forgot. Would you mind if Ames comes to church with my dad and me and then has dinner at the house?"

Dad had finally eased the door back and let Marc inside.

"Dinner?" Mom asked. "How long does your church last?" I could tell from her expression she was imagining snake handling and huge women falling convulsively to the floor while speaking in tongues.

"Sorry, Mrs. Ford. The noon meal on Sunday is still called dinner in this part of Texas. I can have Ames back by two."

"I'll get changed," I said, showing a little Em-style preemptive strike.

I Houdini'd myself into church girl in a ticktock and was back out before Mom could find thirty reasons for me not to go.

Marc opened the passenger door of the truck and helped me in.

"She's watching, isn't she?"

"Both of them," he said. His smile was slow and lazy. He closed my door, walked around the front of the truck, and climbed in, never looking at my parents, never letting them know he was performing.

Let the rumpus, rumpus.

*   *   *

We drove no more than six blocks and turned into a driveway of a house that looked little different from the one I'd just left.

"This is church?"

Marc turned off the ignition and bolted out of the car. As he headed for the door, he shouted over his shoulder. "C'mon."

I opened my own door and followed.

"Like you believed I go to church," Marc said. He unlocked the front door and grabbed my hand, pulling me up to him and kicking the door shut all in one motion. He kissed me urgently and while I tingled, something akin to panic shivered my skin.

It was such a surprise that I didn't really kiss back. Marc lightened the pressure his mouth had on mine, then eased off entirely, quickly kissed the end of my nose, and skimmed his hands up and down my bare arms. *Ohmygod. My first kiss.*

"Whoa, I didn't mean to rush you like that. Sorry." He put his hands in the air as if in mock surrender. "I have to remember just because I'm not a kid, you most certainly still are."

"I'm not a kid," I snapped, just like...well, a kid.

"Are too," he said, stamping his foot like a three-year-old.

"Am not!" I yelled, sticking my tongue out and crossing my eyes. Then I leaned into him and put my arms around him.

"We just had our first fight," Marc said. "You have to pay the toad with a make-up kiss."

"Isn't that pay the *toll*?"

"Maybe." He swept the hair away from my face and leaned down to me. His lips were close, so close, but he didn't touch, he looked, just looked into my eyes. I finally closed the gap and kissed him. My first, official real kiss.

He slid one hand and cupped the back of my head, pulling me to him and teasing my lips with his tongue. A bad-boy kiss. It was as exciting as the gun I'd felt at his ankle the other day.

Spinning and off balance again, I tried to get my

bearings. "Ah, the famous white walls of the Ford Family Rentals."

"I love the look of white in the mornings," Marc said. "By the way, I didn't bring you here to seduce you."

I didn't know if I was disappointed or relieved.

"You didn't? Why not?"

"I brought you here because my dad *is* at church and there's something in my bedroom that you want."

I rolled my eyes at him. "Wow, are you overconfident," I said.

"Don't try to be the tough, sexy chick with me. I don't need her. I need you." Marc leaned his forearms on my shoulders, letting his arms dangle down my back. He kissed my forehead, then rested his forehead against mine. "Hey, do you think because I'm older that I have expectations that you have to fill even if you don't know if you're ready? I'm not that guy."

"I guess I thought you brought me here because...I wondered if..."

"I know," Marc said. He put his index finger on my lips. "Now, shhh."

He grabbed my hand and tugged me along the short hall. What was down there? The guns? His bed? He just said that if I wasn't ready, but maybe...his door was open and on his desk was...

"Oh my gosh, you're wired."

"I figured you had some e-mailing to do," Marc said.

"You are absolutely the best." I landed another sloppy one on him, then planted myself in the chair. "I seriously love you."

"I'll leave you to it," Marc said. "I know you don't want me watching over your shoulder. I need to go start the dinner."

"You cook?"

"I cook."

"Actual *food*? Not just warmed-up takeout?"

"Roast and baked potatoes, but I'll admit the corn is frozen and comes from a bag. But in the summer, it's easy enough to shuck the cobs and boil them."

"Wow. You're amazing," I said. I wasn't kidding, either.

"You're sort of amazing yourself."

"I don't want to be needy and weird, but how am I

amazing? All I've heard lately is how selfish and ungrateful I am. Now there's someone making up my bed, leaving me flowers, bringing me the world through the Internet, and cooking me a real dinner? Why?"

Marc leaned against the door frame. "One thing is that you've got the cool to ask that question. The surface answer is that you're hot." He saw my eye roll. "You asked. Don't argue. Hot. Long legs, long hair, big eyes, smooth skin. Hot. Next, you put up with all your parents' crap and you don't knuckle under. I like that. But you're not hard or mean. You want someone to take care of you. I like that even more. Guys want to protect a woman. Sue me if it makes me feel good to do that. I like how you protect your little sister. That's great."

He stood up, no longer leaning. "But there's something else. I felt like I was steel and you were a magnet. I had a gut feeling I could tell you my secrets and you wouldn't betray me." Now his eyes penetrated mine, and I shivered. "There's something dark in you, Ames, that was searching for the dark in me." He turned and left the room.

Betray him?

Steel and magnets and dark searching for dark?

I guess this could sound all *Wuthering Heights*, but was I getting in over my head? I had to talk to Em.

We were IMing in no time, and I told her everything. Even the gun.

Em was for it. With reservations. "It's time for u to howl at the moon. Remember Tweety?"

I remembered. Time to live by my own rules.

"But make sure it's ur rules and not his. I think u should tell him to keep his guns at home."

I remembered the deep thrill when I touched the handgun strapped to his leg.

"And it's ur game not his. When ur ready to walk, don't listen to that 'u won't betray me' bullcaca. Break it off and shake it off."

"OK," I typed.

Then Em gave me the earthquake news. "I didn't want to tell u. But my p's told yrs u could live with us 'til the end of the school yr. Earl even offered to let u stay on and graduate. Pay ur fees. Ur Mom said no. Dad said ur fees were pd up for this year and it was a waste and we were glad to have u, and it wld increase ur chances of scholar-ship, but no deal. Y'd she do that?"

Because, I thought, *if Mom has to be miserable, so does everyone else.* I was the one she had picked to kick around when things were out of control.

The IM ping brought me out of my trance. Em caught me up on more gossip: She had replaced the cowboy with a punk rock drummer. Her mother was in hysterics but her step coolly brought her more catalogs for prestigious universities.

"Weird," Em wrote. "Rebel thing isn't fun w/o u here. Drummer a bore. I just use him to spin my mom. That's not much fun anymore. My grades r up this week. I get smiley when E says he's proud of me. Frightening."

"Are we switching lives? U liking a dad. Being good grl. Are u going to bcome a Citizen?"

"Nah, not 'til I'm 18 at least."

Em and I finished up and I read my e-mail. There wasn't much. Gone and forgotten from the privileged set.

Marc strolled in and flopped on his bed. "The roast is roasting, the potatoes are doing their thing, and the corn and salad are waiting their turn."

I logged off. I liked this gentler side of Marc, this good-boy side that was making me dinner. But I was ready to know more about his other side, the one that sent chills down my spine.

"So, tell me...what'd you get in trouble for?" I asked. "You know, back when your mom shipped you off here."

Marc's head snapped up, his eyes narrowing. Then he relaxed and laughed softly. "Figured it out, huh? I thought you caught that, even if your parents didn't." He wrapped his arms around me. "It was kid stuff. Joyriding. I totaled a judge's Jag."

"A judge?" I asked. "How unlucky can you be?"

"I knew it was a judge. They have special plates. I didn't think I'd total it. Those babies can get away from you."

His smile was gentle, a caress all its own, and he kissed me on the cheek, then moved to a soft, light kiss on my mouth, and he was pulling me in for a deeper kiss when we heard the front door open.

Marc dropped his hands and I stepped back. "Sit at the computer," he commanded.

I sat and pulled up a Wikipedia article about invertebrates.

"Marc?" The voice was from the hall and eerily like Marc's.

"In the kitchen, Dad. We've got a guest. Ames, take a break from your research and come say hi to my dad."

I headed for the kitchen.

"Ames, meet Marc DeVayne, Sr., my father. Dad, this is Ames Ford."

I put out my hand to shake Mr. DeVayne's, but his eyebrows pinched together and his mouth hardened into a line. He didn't take his eyes off me as he said, "Marc, I need to talk to you, privately."

I dropped my outstretched hand, confused. Marc placed iced tea on the table. "Ames, have some tea. Dad and I will chat outside. No worries."

He and his father hurried out the back door, but it didn't pull completely shut. Like with our back door, the humidity had warped the wood and a sliver of air let their words sneak into the house.

"Marc, how old is that girl?"

"Dad, don't go ballistic. She—"

"This is a repeat of what happened before. You know better. If she's sixteen I'll give a party. But I'll lay odds she's not. What are you thinking, bringing her here? Alone?"

"I brought her to meet you. To have a Sunday meal with us."

"Get her out of here. Do not see her again. I mean it, Marc."

"I'm old enough to make my own decisions," Marc said.

"Get a job, get an apartment, and you can get in any kind of trouble you want. Live here, and you stay out of trouble. That was the deal. Now take her home."

Marc came back in. He didn't look angry. He looked smug. "I cooked dinner for him. That's the thanks I get. I guess you heard it all?"

"Yes," I said. "Let's go."

As he drove me home, I asked, "What did your father mean when he said this was a repeat of what happened before?"

"I don't know what he wants me to do," Marc said. "He thinks I shouldn't be dating girls that are that much younger than I really am." He shrugged then sighed. "I had a couple of dates with a girl that was sixteen and he blew up just like he did today. I think he just wants to fight so I'll get out of his house."

"Why don't you leave then? Getting a job has to be better than putting up with him."

When he slid his eyes to me his face was flushed, his voice a warning. "I thought you of all people would get it. He abandoned me. Wouldn't even visit for years. Now I'm here. I'm going to remind him of every minute he made me miserable."

"That's why you want me?" I bristled. "You're using me to make him miserable?"

"Pull your claws back in, Tiger. Don't say you aren't using me to rub in your parents' faces. But go figure, we click."

I let my breath out. Of course he was right. He had been a pawn on my chessboard until, well, I guess until he kissed me.

If I was supposed to be the one in control, why didn't it feel that way?

ART AND ANGER

Marc turned when he saw the bright lights and the cartoon colors of Whataburger. "I did promise you supper. It's your turn now. Tell me what happened. Everything."

Unlike anyone else lately, Marc wanted to know about me. So over fries, Cokes, and burgers—he kicked them back old school, with ketchup, like I did (no cheese or chili or, the horror, mustard)—I told him the whole story. Dad's job, the stealing, the bailout, the gambling, the grandparents, my shoplifting, being left in jail, the plan, how the plan collapsed in a day—the whole mess. He never looked bored. He soaked up every word.

"You know your dad will never get another job, right?"

I put down my burger. "Well, yeah, in Colorado. That's why we left, but he says that in Houston..."

Marc shook his head. Slow. "Nope. He was fired with cause. His old place won't tell what he did, but they won't give a recommendation. No other place will touch him. He won't be able to be a greeter at a Wal-Mart."

"Whoa, don't be such a downer. He could work at a bookstore or, geez, he could work here slinging burgers. They hire anybody."

"Ames, he can't be trusted around money. That's what's going to be in his file. He may as well be radioactive."

Radioactive. Yes. That's how I'd felt in school. The fear gripped me again. I felt the fries turn sour. But I didn't want to be that weepy, needy girl. "What're you telling me? My time in the slums is not temporary? That I should learn to love poverty?"

I fought for a silly grin. "I have need of those

Victorian-type words. Alas and alack. I feel a swoon coming on." I put the back of my hand to my forehead.

"Good try," Marc said. "Your mom has to get a job. Do you have a college fund that he didn't get into?"

I sobered. "No. He raided everything to keep from being arrested."

I'd known that fact for a little while, but the reality had never sunk in. I wasn't going to college. This... hopelessness was not temporary. It was my future.

"That's lousy. I'm really sorry." He looked up at the clock. "We have to get moving."

"It's not two yet," I said.

"Always bring 'em back early. Don't give the parents any room for hatin'," Marc quipped.

I tilted my head and pointed a finger at Marc. "You sound far too experienced with all this. Too much technique."

"I spend a lot of time in front of the TV. That's my dad's idea of home-schooling." He put on a mock California surfer dude accent. "What's with the hatin', dude? It's all good."

"That's so old," I said.

"Texans don't know that. As long as we're making fun of Californians—anything goes." Then he stuck out his tongue at me. Just as I had done earlier. I laughed. How could I not?

When he pulled up in front of the house he got out and opened the door for me. "No swappin' spit in front of the audience."

"Which we have?" I asked.

"No doubt."

I smiled at him. He closed the car door and leaned against it. "I had a great time. Tell your dad I'll be here tomorrow to clear out all the weeds and overgrown shrubs."

"Thanks for dinner," I said. "I'll tell him." I bounced up the sidewalk.

Mom and Dad had one of our old rugs down and had saved a sofa and chair from the basement. Dad was putting an Ikea coffee table together. The lush rug teamed with the gross couch and the Danish-type table on the peeling linoleum was hideous. It highlighted everything that was wrong about the house. Talk about nowhere to go. My sense of claustrophobia ratcheted up to about the power of three.

"Fire the decorator. He's either not really gay or on the wrong kind of drugs," I said.

"Lovely," Mom said. "We're doing our best and you flit off for a morning of fun and come back just as smart-mouthed as ever. We really appreciate it."

Mom and I stared each other down for a long minute, then Chrissy ran into the room waving a piece of paper. "I made us ART."

Chrissy had drawn a picture of a fish a bit crookedly on the paper and colored in arced stripes yellow, blue, purple, red, green, practically every bright color in her crayon box. "It's a rainbow trout!" she announced. "To remind us of Colorado."

She trotted over to the wall behind the sofa and taped the picture against the wall. It beat Mom's trendy new artists from the overpriced galleries.

"A rainbow? That's really something, Chrissy," Dad said.

Mom patted Chrissy's head and stretched out an arm to pluck the picture from the wall. I stepped sideways to block her path.

She wanted control of those walls, but she was going to hurt Chrissy's feelings over my entirely dead and cold body. I could see in her eyes that she knew that.

She dropped her hand.

"Ames," Mom snapped. "You might have noticed there isn't a washer or dryer here. That means you'll need to go to a place you've never experienced before: a Laundromat. I think that's a perfect job for you."

Mom had lost our skirmish over Chrissy's picture, but she made sure I left bleeding.

Monday morning, Mom left without a word. I gathered all the dirty clothes and when Dad and Marc took a break, I carried a glass of iced tea out to Marc as he chatted with Chrissy under the scraggly tree.

"I know this is going to be irritating and I'm going to sound rich-girl stupid..." I prefaced.

"I'm not going to teach you to tie your shoes," Marc joked.

I used our move. I stuck my tongue out at him.

"You know how to wash clothes?" I asked.

"I cook, I clean, I wash," he said. "Full service." He winked over Chrissy's head.

"Tell me." I had a small notebook and a pen. "Steps, in order."

"Gotcha. Gather clothes. Separate."

I wrote it down, but I looked up with my eyebrows bunched in a question.

"Yeah, I thought that meant put everything that went in one drawer together. Mistake."

I smiled. "I'm not quite *that* stupid."

"Neither was I, duh."

"Then..." The light, as they say, dawned. "I'm such a bonehead. You said that to make me feel better. About not knowing how to do something so..." I searched for a word.

"Fundamental." Marc supplied it. "Yeah. It's not your

fault no one taught you how. You shouldn't have to feel like a moron about it."

I couldn't look at him. I had the all-over warm fuzzies and was smiling like a . . . big ol' . . . girlie girl.

"So, the wash," Marc said. Pulling me back to reality.

"You put stuff that's alike in one washing machine. Towels together. Dark colors can't go with light colors. The dryers are really hot so take your clothes out slightly damp. Don't let 'em dry to the bone. It ruins the T-shirts and shrinks everything. Especially your delicate stuff— make sure you don't put 'em in the dryer."

I wrote as fast as I could. "These aren't steps," I complained.

"Yeah, they are. I'm just not numbering them for you. Learn to adjust."

I let out a loud sigh and pushed my hair behind my ear. "You sound just like *them*."

His hand shot out before I took another breath. No other part of his body moved. His face was shuttered. The notebook ripped from my hand and sailed across the yard. He got up and walked to the house.

"I'm ready to get back to work, Mr. Ford. Take all the time you need."

I gaped after him. Stunned at the quickness and the...violence.

"I don't think anybody should ever make him mad," Chrissy said.

"No," I said. "I guess not."

HEROES

When Dad picked me up at the Laundromat he was hot and cranky. "I'm too old and out of shape for this," he said. "I'm taking tomorrow off. You and Marc can work on cutting the yard back. I'm going to see about getting a phone and your mother can be damned. We're getting basic cable and DSL. I need a real job and I can't do it with dial-up."

I clenched my fists. He didn't care that I might be tired and needed a day off, but I didn't want to start a fight. Hey, he was going to get DSL—the tiniest part of my real life back. Better yet, he was giving me time to talk to Marc alone. I couldn't keep my head straight since he had walked away from me.

"The laundry smells great," Dad said. "You, however, smell like cigarettes."

"I know. There's a jillion No Smoking signs and people sit right underneath them puffing away," I said.

"Reminds me of my parents. They complain they don't have money for food, but they smoke cigarettes. People don't have a washer and dryer—they could buy one with what they spend on smokes."

I couldn't believe him—all holier-than-thou over cigarettes? What about the money he spent on beer and Jack Daniel's? Or, how about, *we don't have a house anymore because you stole and gambled*?

We got home and I slammed my way inside. I tossed my parents' clothes on their bed and took the rest of the stuff to my room, where Marc was playing with Chrissy.

"Shhh, the bears have worked hard and are taking a nap. I just sang them a lullaby," Marc said.

"His singing is so bad they fainted," Chrissy reported.

Marc hung his head then looked at me through his eyelashes. "I'm sorry. I've been punished for my bad behavior."

"I detentioned him," Chrissy said.

"Oh, that's why you're in here," I grumbled.

"Yes, I'm, uh, *bear*sitting while your dad went to pick you up."

"He means babysitting me, but he's trying to be nice now," Chrissy said.

"Gotcha." A wisp of smile snagged my mouth.

He tilted his head toward the hall as he stood. We went out together.

"I blew up. Sorry, I didn't like being compared to your parents. I don't like to think I treat you like they do."

"You don't. It was stupid, I…"

I couldn't finish. His lips were on mine. Soft, sweet, quick. Leaving me wanting more.

But we were interrupted by the slam of the front door. I scooted into the bedroom with Chrissy, and Marc slid into the bathroom, closed the door, and flushed.

Mom came into the hall as Marc came out of the bathroom. "Sorry, Mrs. Ford. Mind if I get some cold water then go back to work?"

Mom flicked her eyes over him. "If you don't mind, I need some help with the rug in the front room."

She leaned into the doorway. "Ames, you too. Let's roll up this rug. I've found a place to sell it. Marc, I'd like to talk to you about this home-schooling thing. I went to the high school today and didn't like what I saw. Home-schooling might be just the thing for Ames."

I got up and followed them into the front room. Marc moved the ridiculous coffee table. The three of us got on our knees to roll up and sell off the last bit of luxury.

"Keep it in a tight roll. Roll the rug to you, don't roll to the rug," Mom said, always the Commander.

"So what did you see that was so bad, a mugging?"

"Practically. I was there less than two hours and I saw two fights. I walked through the halls during class changes and I simply couldn't believe the language those children used."

I glanced at Marc. Mom should have taken a stroll through the halls of my pricey school. Her hair would've stood on end. Did she think because we wore Peter Pan collars that we didn't swear?

"One couple was kissing and crawling all over each other. Let's just say that if there's a baby in nine months, I think I witnessed conception."

Marc laughed. A big, boisterous laugh, like it was surprised out of him.

Mom sat back on her heels. "I am not making a joke. These two were coiled about each other up against the lockers and writhing like snakes on hot pavement. A teacher did break it up. But it might have been too late." This time she and Marc both laughed. Mom's was tentative at first, then a little louder and more carefree.

Why did I hate this? Marc and my mother laughing together? I knew he was working her, but...

"So, exactly how am I supposed to make friends if I don't go to school?" My tone smothered the mood.

"I made friends." Marc shrugged. "It's easy enough."

"That's one of the things I want to ask Marc about,"

Mom said. Her angry face was back in place. "This isn't a punishment, Ames."

"Let's just get the rug done." I rolled.

"Ames, I said you bring it to you, not push it away."

It was easier to push.

Just as we finished, Dad came in with a set of phones, a bag of wires and some Cat-5 stuff, a cable box, and, surprise, another six-pack. "Marc, can you help me set this stuff up?" He turned to me. "You've still got the wireless thing for your laptop and your printer, right?"

I nodded.

"We're in business," Dad said.

Mom's body looked like it vibrated. "The only thing that's changed is geography. I guess you just blew all the money I got for the rug." She banged out of the house and the car roared out of the drive.

"I didn't ask her to sell the rug," Dad complained.

I stood there, not quite knowing which way to look.

"Ames, I thought you were supposed to be clearing the weeds from around the house. Why are you standing here? Get to work. Do I have to do everything?"

My head exploded. "No, you've done plenty already."

I saw the bag of wires he held coming toward my face then, and my eyelids mashed together, bracing for the hit. It never came.

I opened my eyes, and Marc held Dad's wrist.

"You need to calm down, Mr. Ford. You don't want to be hitting your daughter."

Dad jerked his arm away from Marc. "You need to mind your own business." But he walked away, dumping his stuff on the sofa. I heard him open the fridge, thump down the new six-pack, and crack open a can.

Marc whispered to me. "Go play with Chrissy." His voice was soft. His eyes were not.

I sprouted wings. Someone had taken up for me. Had protected me. While Em had always been on my side, she had never gone toe-to-toe with my parents like Marc just had. "That's the second time," I said.

"What?"

"He almost hit me before. In Colorado. He stopped himself that time. I don't think he would have this time."

Marc put his hand to my cheek and ran his thumb over my lips. "Now go close your door, let him mellow. I'll hook up the cable and the computers and we can work on the yard when it's cooler."

I was a mess. Rage toward my father overwhelmed me but I was lovestunned by Marc. I went to Chrissy's room. Just like I'd been told.

Later, I joined Marc outside and we hacked at the overgrown shrubs and vines that grew ragged and wild close to the house.

"You whack them and I'll walk them to the curb," I said.

He chopped and I carted and we didn't talk much. Dad stayed in the house on the computer; I could see him watch us from the window from time to time.

We worked the shrubbery all the way around the house, and I was introduced to the mysteries of Saint Augustine grass. There was no grass like this in Boulder. This was warrior grass. It grew in long runners with a death grip on the ground that would take a sumo wrestler to pry loose.

We knelt next to each other, struggling to rip the grass from the ground.

"Marc, there's something I want to tell you."

"This sounds serious," he said.

"Good serious, I think."

"Good is...well..." He grinned. "Good."

I took a deep breath. "I used to think my dad was my hero. As corny as it sounds. I don't know any other word. It's been a real wake-up call finding how stupid I've been about that. But my hero's not Dad. It's...you."

Marc sat back and pulled me into his lap. He kissed me. I kissed him back. Then kissed him again.

"Ames!" I felt Dad's shadow first, but his voice startled me anyway. I jumped, but Marc kept me in his lap.

"Ames, get off that boy this minute."

"Mr. Ford, we're not doing anything wrong. We're out here in front of God and everybody. It was just a kiss," Marc said, still holding me.

"Get up, Ames. Now." Marc released me and we both stood.

"Dad—"

"Shut up and go in the house."

I grabbed Marc's hand and held on. "Get over yourself, Dad. It's not like I haven't kissed anyone before." Well, I had. I'd kissed Marc before.

"You're fifteen years old," Dad roared.

"Sixteen soon enough. Dad, this is not a big deal. Why are you so—"

"Go in the house." He lowered his voice, but his anger strummed.

"Ames, go ahead. Your dad and I need to talk." Marc squeezed my hand and let it go. His voice was lazy and smooth. But his eyes were hooded. Cobra eyes.

Fifteen minutes after I went into the house, Dad stalked into my room. His fury was tamped down—somewhat—but he seemed to have grown a spine.

"Ames, whatever is going on with Marc is over. You are too young for a relationship like that." He ran his hand through his hair and sighed. "Wasn't Emily enough to show you what damage early sexual experience does to a girl? Is that what you want for yourself? As a role model for Chrissy?"

Translation: Don't embarrass us. Don't mess up Chrissy, the good kid.

I stared past him and willed him to drop dead on the spot.

"Marc admitted he's too old for you. Too experienced. I'm sorry I tried to grab you, but this..." He flipped his palms up and looked around the pathetic room. "This whole situation...it's turned me into someone I don't even recognize. Everything fell apart. I don't even know how it all started."

He didn't know how it started? Take a little responsibility.

"Anyway, Marc will still work here until the house is done. But he's agreed there will be no physical contact between you. None. I want you to agree to it, too."

"What if I don't?"

Dad looked as stunned as if I'd slapped *him*.

"Ames?"

"What? You can't beat me or tie me up or watch me

every minute of the day. Now get out of my room. I don't talk to drunks."

Dad looked like someone punched a hole in him and let all the air out. His face drained of color and he looked old and frail. He left the room like he was lost.

I caught a movement from the corner of my eye. I turned to see the open closet door. Chrissy was sitting in the closet, arranging her bears in rows.

She didn't look at me.

When Marc arrived the next day he went to work scraping the front of the house while I worked on the back. I didn't talk to him and he didn't talk to me, but I didn't believe Dad's story. Marc was full of double-talk. He'd tell Dad what he wanted to hear and have another plan of his own.

Marc didn't try to meet me in secret. Didn't say anything all day other than it was getting hotter. Insomnia-curing conversation. As he was leaving at six, Mom rolled in. She looked tired but smug.

"I got a job. A receptionist at a dentist office. I make

appointments, file insurance claims, that kind of thing."
She plopped down on the couch. "My résumé is skimpy,
but my interview convinced him that I could do what
needed to be done. The thing I do best is organize,
right?"

"I thought you were thinking about home-schooling
the kids?" Dad said.

She looked at Dad like he was a slug. "I think we need
to put some food on the table. You'll do the home-
schooling while you search for your 'perfect job.'" She
rose and strode past Dad. "See to dinner, will you? I'm
going to take a shower."

Power shift. Complete parental chaos. Strangers.

"Forget that. She can go hungry," Dad said, and
shambled to the little table that held his computer and
booted up.

I guess that meant Chrissy and I could go hungry,
too. I dragged myself to the kitchen and made a box of
mac and cheese. I took two hot bowls to our bedroom,
my raw palms suddenly feeling blistered by the heat, and
handed Chrissy a bowl. She was on the bed braiding a

stuffed horse's mane. Where'd that come from?

"I love it when it's gooey. Mom makes it too dry and Dad makes it too runny."

I put my bowl on the nightstand and flopped on the bed. There was a lump under my pillow. I lifted my head and pulled out a cell phone. The prepaid, throwaway kind. I turned it on. One programmed number.

Marc.

One voice message.

Marc.

Meet me at midnight at the end of the block. My dad works the late shift tonight. I won't let your dad keep us apart. I won't let him hurt you, either.

Chrissy watched me delete the message. I watched her braid the horse's mane.

"Did Marc give you that cute little horse?"

She nodded. "He said he had secret presents for both of us."

"Secret presents?"

"Yes, he said not to tell Mom and Dad because it will

make them sad because they can't afford to give us presents right now," Chrissy said.

This guy was a great liar.

I grinned at that. Then my grin vanished.

This guy was a great liar.

I shook it off.

ET TU, BRUTE

The household was snoring like a bear's den by ten thirty, so I slipped into the so-called family room to use the phone.

"Ames, do *not* tell me they have phones in Texas." Em sounded like the old Em. "Is it, like, a civilized state or do you have cattle in the kitchen?"

I tried to laugh. "What's up in the real world?"

"I've given up guys," Em said.

I was jolted off my feet by the fact that the earth had just stopped rotating. "Do not mess with my head, Em. My life is insane enough."

Em sighed. "I'm serious. Dad made me a deal." This was new. Em had never called a step by anything but his first name.

"Earl bribed you into not having sex?"

"Not exactly. Well, okay, exactly. Here's the deal: If I don't have a boyfriend during the summer, then I can work for him during break. Not like in the mail room, but seeing how cases work. I can go with him to the courtroom." Her voice was rapid fire and excited. "I upped the ante and said, 'Let's start now.' I didn't do much of anything but hand him stuff and put stuff back in order, but I get a peek at criminal law that nobody my age gets. He just wants me to see if something besides sex could interest me. Show me that I might be good at something else."

Who was this on the phone? Where was my friend that barked at fences just because they were there?

"What happened to the rebel for any cause? I thought the boy toys were how you got control."

"Dad thinks I'm worth more than...well, he cares. He says I'm using guys as a Band-Aid. For all the shrinks I've been to, Earl makes sense. And he hasn't left."

My stomach hurt. I had to sit down.

"Ames, you're not saying anything."

"Yeah," I finally managed. "Earl's a good guy."

"Forget it," Em said. "If a hot body shows on the horizon I'll probably go back to my old ways. But with nothing else going on, talking cases with Dad is interesting."

"You've called him 'Dad' three times."

"Did I? Well, he's more of a dad to me than that sperm donor ever was. Anyway, what's up with you?"

A smile spread over my face along with a flush. "I have a boyfriend. I'm going to meet him at midnight."

"The old guy?"

"He's not old. He's twenty-two."

"Six years' difference. Too much."

What was this crap? Coming from her? "You've dated guys that much older."

"I've been around the block. You haven't even walked next door alone." She paused. "Ames, you know how everybody on the planet thought I was the bad influence and you had it all together?"

"Right, but it was never like that," I said.

"You know why?"

"Sure, I like your wild side. You were doing the things I didn't have the nerve to do."

"Nope," Em said. "Think about it. I know how to keep from getting in too deep. You get started and keep going. You can't self-correct. I had to do that for you. Now I'm not there."

"I can't 'self-correct'? Is this one of your old shrinks talking or Earl? It sure isn't the Em I used to know."

"The Em you used to know is so yesterday."

I couldn't, wouldn't believe what I was hearing. Em was practically entering a nunnery.

Em cleared her throat and did the singsong thing. "So-ooooo, why are you meeting him at midnight?"

"Guess."

"Oopsie. You aren't allowed to date him. Do they know how old he is?"

"Dad thinks he's seventeen and he thinks that's too old. I think he can think whatever he wants."

"Tick, tock—we've traded personalities. So, sneaky slut, have you done the deed?"

I was quiet for a minute. Em's tone was teetering on the edge of, what exactly, disapproval?

"Not yet."

"Good, hold off for a while. You want to make sure *you're* the user in the relationship—not him."

"Why should either of us be a user?" Anger tinged my tone.

"Don't get pissy."

"He protects me."

A groan from Em. "From what? You can't be this... well, this stupid."

That was it. "You have *no* idea what this is like, Em. You have no freaking clue."

"I'm trying to help you, Tweety. I don't know everything about your parents' shit, sure, but I know the type of guy who likes younger girls. Does he give you orders? Get mad when he doesn't have control?"

I didn't say anything.

"Hello?"

I hung up.

*   *   *

I looked at the clock. It was only eleven thirty but I was ready to get out of this ugly, claustrophobic excuse of a house. I walked right out the front door.

Not a block away the lights flashed from a parked car. I stopped and they flashed again. Marc? This early? He stepped out of the truck and I ran the rest of the way.

He grabbed me around the waist, swinging me in a circle as he kissed me.

"You're early," I breathed.

"I left as soon as Dad did. I didn't want you out in this neighborhood alone."

My hero hustled me into the truck.

"When do your parents wake up?"

"They aren't the problem. Chrissy wakes up around six."

"Okay, you'll be back by five. Does that work?" He took his eyes from the ignition switch and searched my face.

I returned his gaze and smiled. "That's perfect."

GENTLING THE HORSE

It wasn't perfect.

It started out all dreamy and moody and sweet, but then...it was invasive. I pulled back, but Marc held me down and whispered that it would be fine. It wasn't. It hurt. Pushing, jabbing, shoving. I grit my teeth and turned my head away, but Marc didn't seem to notice. His eyes were closed tight. I don't think it mattered who was there. As long as someone was there.

But when it was over, he was all Marc again, kind and smiling. "I know, I know, sweetheart. It hurt and you hated it. It's always like that the first time. It's just something you have to get over with. It's so unfair that it's like that for girls." He curled me into him and smoothed my hair. Covered my face with soft kisses. "Next time will be so much easier. So sweet. You'll see."

I got back home at five and crawled into bed. I still hurt a little. The sex itself was kind of awful, but the after was wonderful. When another person looks at you like there's nothing before you and nothing beyond...that's what made it worth it to me.

One thing was certain. Being bad was easier than I'd ever realized. I had always thought Em was lucky or her parents were stupid or uncaring. The reality was that anyone could do it.

Over the next two weeks I kept the cell on vibrate and Marc texted. *Love you, Marc.*

Or *Text me.*

Tell me everything you are doing.

I hate having you out of my sight.

Make me a word picture.

Whenever I went to do the laundry we talked.

"Your dad is watching us like a hawk. I couldn't talk to you at all today," Marc said when he called at two in the morning.

"I know. I have blisters from scraping the paint off the house. I told Dad tonight that I either need to register for school or he needs to let me set up home-schooling and study during the day."

"Yeah. This work is too much for you. It was fine to keep putting it off as long as we could talk and touch each other, but now...I'd rather know you're not breaking your back, even if it means I can only watch you through the windows."

"I wish this was a camera phone so I could have a picture of you," I said.

A snapshot of Marc appeared under my pillow the next night.

I snuck out nights to see him. Sometimes just for a few minutes. Sometimes to go to his house. For sex and then for cuddling and talk, and sometimes just for cuddling and talk. Once he showed me a documentary about a prison work program that had inmates training horses.

"They did that at juvie, too," Marc said. "For us older inmates." He snorted. "I was gonna do it until they said that after we got the horse trained, it was given away."

I knew better than to say anything.

"I told them to forget it. Once I make something mine, nobody takes it from me. Nobody."

"I wouldn't want to break a horse anyway," I said. "It seems cruel."

"You don't break them," Marc said. "That's the old way. Now, you gentle them. Works lots better."

What did it matter? In the end the horse still didn't have a choice. I sighed and leaned against his chest. Marc tightened his arm around me.

On another night, his dad was home, so we were curled up together in his truck. "Tell me about it," I said. "Why you're here. How they hurt you so much."

"You know most of it," Marc said.

I shrugged in his arms. "I know isolated facts."

"Dad bailed. I don't know, I took that...personally. I

felt like he left me. Didn't want me. It was like someone took away my anchor."

I took his hand and laced my fingers through.

"I did stupid stuff, getting attention. Skipping school, shoplifting. Name some random kid kind of destructiveness and I probably did it. Nobody noticed. Or cared. Mom was worried about paying the bills and the younger kids. Dad had checked out and wasn't checking back in."

He sighed and raked his fingers through his hair. "So I went big and boosted a car. Got caught. I thought Dad would come rescue me and Mom would cry and..." He stopped. "They didn't even get me a real lawyer. Public defender. They turned their backs on me. Abandoned me."

"That's horrible."

"I hate them both," Marc said.

His voice wasn't angry. It was cold, unflinching. I had the thought that he was more dangerous than his gun. I pushed that away. We had a pact. He was just a hurt boy.

OWNERSHIP

The party was the beginning of the end.

"This is a party for, ummm, 'marginals,'" Marc warned me as we drove out to the house where the party was taking place. "There's goths, punks, tweakers, tokers, bikers, the way-out art crowd, and a few seriously mentals. What there aren't are frats, teen queens, Bible thumpers, or anybody that thinks they are somebody. These people live on the edge of the map—where there be dragons."

"We're here because?"

"I have a deal to make."

"What kind of deal?" I asked.

"That's my business. Here comes my guy. You stay quiet. Got it?"

A wave of irritation swamped me, but I was out of my element and I knew better than to make Marc mad.

A guy that looked like a cartoon bad guy slouched up. Long, thin greasy hair. Leather vest, dirty jeans, bad teeth, gleaming shark teeth on leather thongs around his neck, miles of tats. Couldn't he just cut the crap and pin "I am a serious badass" on his shirt?

"You got it?" Marc asked.

"In the back. Got my stuff?"

Marc tilted his head.

"Sorry, I know, man of your word and all that. C'mon."

Marc took my hand and towed me through the crowd.

"The chick doesn't come," the badass cartoon man growled.

The *chick*? Couldn't help it. I laughed.

"Somethin' funny?"

Marc glared at me. I tried for composure.

"She's with me. She comes," Marc said.

"Then it's on you," Cartoon Man said.

He turned his back and led the way. When his vest hiked up, I saw the gun tucked into his waistband. He wasn't funny anymore.

In the bathroom of the dilapidated house, the man shoved back the moldy shower curtain. Then he pulled up a black tarp. Displayed on a plywood board were handguns. He picked that up and balanced it across the toilet. Another black tarp. When that came up there were two guns. Shotguns. Sawed off. Completely illegal.

My skin shivered. This wasn't a handgun snapped into an ankle holster. Marc had said he had a gun collection. I pictured a rifle, a shotgun. I blew out a calming breath. Get real here, Ames. You knew there had to be something illegal. There wasn't a gun cabinet in his house. No display. You knew. What's different about a sawed-off shotgun? A shotgun is a shotgun, right?

Marc picked one up. He held it down along his side and jacked it with one hand. Then again.

He looked at the man.

"It'll blow a hole in an elephant. Get up close and it's over, Grover."

Marc's smile was eerie. "I love her."

Love her? Something flashed through me. Jealousy?

He reached into his jacket pocket and produced a large baggie and a wad of cash.

The man counted the cash, then opened the bag and sniffed. "Smells righteous. I got your word this is good shit?"

Marc's face hardened and the cobra eyes flashed. He handed the sawed-off shotgun to the man. "If you've ever had so much as a stem, one stem, and the weed hasn't been mind-busting, you shoot me in the head, right here, right now."

There wasn't much room to back up in the filthy bathroom, so I was pressed against the wall. Marc was...lethal.

Shark handed the shotgun back and put his hands up. "Go home, dude. Chill."

"I'll go home when I'm ready. My woman wants to dance."

I didn't want to dance. I wanted to go home and crawl under the bed, but that was the old Ames. This was the Ames who howled and prowled and lunged at the throats of anyone who annoyed her. The Ames who wanted to be Marc's "woman."

In the main room of the house I saw a girl with a black leather biker's vest swinging open and unbuttoned with nothing underneath but skin. She was dancing by herself to the music. Marc swept past me. "Back in a few."

He left me alone. With these "marginal" people. Because of that gun. The one he *loved*.

The black vest girl stopped with a stagger. "You look lost." She pointed, her wrist and fingers limp, a vague wave. "The party bowl's on the coffee table. Take a handful and get right."

I looked around. There were men here, not boys. They watched me, vulturelike. I smiled to myself. Power. It rushed through me and tingled at my fingertips and lips. If my parents had that feeling of power over me, no wonder they didn't want to give it up.

I walked over to the party bowl. Pills of every kind. Mix and match. Marc showed up beside me. "The idea is to grab a handful and wash it down. Nobody gets the same combination."

"I'm not four. I know how it works. But somebody ends up in the emergency room and I'm not looking for that to be me," I said.

Marc smiled, then kissed me. "I had to learn that the hard way. How old are you again?"

"Young enough for bad to be fun and old enough to know that you have to practice to be really bad enough."

I pulled out of his embrace and started a swaying dance, my hands over my head. Let the men with the vultures' eyes look. Let Marc be a little jealous when he saw other men want his *woman*. Then he'd see who he loved—me or a shotgun.

Marc's smile straightened out, his lips thin and tight, like...almost like my mother's when she disapproved.

I shimmied up to him and then away. I didn't care about the watchers now. I was caught up in the music, relaxing to the beat, to the pulse of the other writhing bodies in the room. I lifted my hair off my neck and—

"Stop that! People are looking at you. Stop making a slut of yourself." He grabbed one of my uplifted arms and yanked it down, then he pulled me along behind him, out to his car.

He drove me home in silence and stopped at the corner. When, shocked and confused, I didn't get out, waiting for him to say something or at least come around and open my door as he usually had, he reached across my body and pushed open my door. Then he shoved my shoulder, hard. He had the element of surprise and I slid out onto the street, landing hard, the pebbles on the side of the road gouging my cheek. Marc floored the truck and the door swung shut, missing my cocked-up knee by what seemed an inch and flinging more road gravel onto me.

I pushed up into a sitting position and inspected the

cuts and scrapes, too dazed to feel any emotion, too dazed to see the cruelty. All I could think was: What had I done? Why was he so angry?

Marc was all I had. I wasn't ready for him to push me away.

I slowly got up, testing my knees and ankles and brushing dirt away from my clothes when I heard the truck. Then I was bathed in the glare of his headlights. I felt my heart slow down. Like my life was banging to the adagio beat of a loud drum. Would he run me over?

Marc jumped out of the truck with the motor still running. I flinched when he threw his arms around me.

"What is *wrong* with me? I'm so sorry. Ames. Please, please. I love you, baby. I just got so jealous when I saw those guys looking at you. You were so beautiful and sexy when you were dancing and it's like my head exploded."

He pulled back and looked at me, stroking my face with his thumbs. His thick-lashed eyes were deep with tears. "I'm a jerk. I know it. I'm not going to be one again. I swear."

He kissed me, little kisses, all over my face, then my neck, then long deep kisses on the mouth. He led me back to the idling truck and shoved me down into the seats, fumbling with my clothes and his. The sex was rough, fast and painful, but it was what I had to hold him close to me.

FALLING

The next night I called Marc. I knew he was still in apology mode and I could get pretty much what I wanted. I didn't want to be shoved around anymore. I wanted more control. I needed to be more important than those guns.

"Pick me up at midnight. It's time I see your gun collection," I told him.

"Cool. You'll love it." He sounded relieved that I had called. Excited that I wanted to see his treasure.

When we got to his house he tugged me straight to his

closet. He opened the door, leaned forward, and pulled a chain that hung from the ceiling. A light flicked on and he pushed the clothes apart, revealing a plywood panel. He swung it open.

I involuntarily sucked in my breath. "Jesus!"

Guns, knives. More guns. Handguns. Rifles. Shotguns. All different kinds.

I didn't know much more than a cap gun from a cannon, but I think there was everything except a cannon in there. One looked like those machine-gun things you see drug runners use on TV.

One handgun had been a turn-on. This was overwhelming.

"Planning a war?" I asked, trying not to let on how much my head was reeling. Considering the firepower here, a massacre wasn't out of the realm of possibility.

His eyes almost glazed over. He was dreaming standing up. His smile was small but satisfied. It both chilled and excited me.

"Kind of like that. I think of creeping people's houses while they sleep. Going into their bedroom and standing over them with my gun. I have the power. All the power and they don't even know. I could take everything from them. Everything. Life. And they sleep."

He clicked off the light and closed the door. "I think about it all the time. I'm going to do it soon. I am. The ultimate thrill."

Ultimate thrill. Yes. I shivered as that dark thing inside me crawled up my neck, trying to take hold. But the sheer number of guns shoved it down again. I backed away from him.

Then I ran.

I pounded out of Marc's house and down the broken sidewalks. I ran for two blocks before I was winded and lost. All the houses looked alike. I wasn't sure if I had turned in the right direction when I had bolted from the house.

Marc's truck pulled up alongside me. "Ames, wait. Please."

I didn't look at him and willed my feet forward as fast as I could.

"Ames, get in the truck. I'll drive you home. I just want to explain."

"Are you going to shoot me, or just let me know that you *can* any time you want?"

He slammed the truck into park and jumped out of it, leaving it running. He sprinted toward me and I poured on more speed. I couldn't outrun him. He grabbed my shoulder and spun me to face him.

"I'm not carrying. I swear. I saw you were freaked. That's what took me a couple of minutes to follow. Check me." He raised both hands palms out.

I kicked his ankles. Nothing there. "Turn around." I slapped the waistband of his jeans. Again, nothing.

I took a giant step away from him and folded my arms across my chest.

"Can I talk?"

No answer. No reaction. I stared off to the left. Away from the charm.

He sighed. "Okay. I moved way too fast. But you did ask to see the guns. I guess I didn't understand how much you've been betrayed. They must have spun your world so hard, you lost all footing."

I sneaked a quick glance at him.

"It's not so much that you can't trust me. It's that you have trust issues with just about anybody. Here I go talking about creeping around.... But don't you see, showing you all this, the guns, telling you my secret, was my way of giving you power."

My jaw loosened.

"You control me now, and I know it. All this gives me the way to take care of you. How can anyone hurt you again if I'm there with the ability to let them live and make them die?"

I looked at him now.

"Don't make up your mind yet. Come back with me. We won't talk about guns. I'll earn your trust. I'll get to know you better. Find out all the Ames stuff I don't know. Okay? You don't have to do anything you don't want to. But never think I'll hurt you. That's not going to happen."

Marc's eyes bore into mine. Liars can't look you straight in the face, right? Not like he was.

"Okay," I said. "But I'm not promising anything."

I went back with him. We talked. *He* talked. And he

talked. He didn't break me. He gentled me. He called the dark thing in me. He sang its song.

The next day we were sanding the metal window grates in preparation for painting. Dad was on the computer and, being a man of no follow-through, he occasionally left Marc and me alone together.

We sanded in silence but I finally sighed, dusted off my hands, and spoke to the air in front of me.

"I'm sorry about running out of the house and all that drama."

He stopped sanding. Listened.

"I won't tell anyone about what I saw. I understand how it makes you feel safe. Sometimes you need something...*outside* of yourself to feel safe." I felt like I was talking to myself now. "Something kind of dangerous and bigger than you. Something you've never had experience with before. Because everything and everybody you know has let you down."

I turned to look at him. I was shocked—I could swear that Marc had tears in his eyes. He waved me off—as if telling me not to try to comfort him—then nodded for me to continue.

I waited a second or two. Yanked up a handful of grass. "So, your secret is safe. I want you to protect me. I need that."

Marc didn't respond.

"My parents abandoned me, so I promise not to do that to you. But there's two things I want you to promise me."

He ground the sandpaper against a metal bar. "Okay."

"You don't know what they are," I said.

"It doesn't matter. Whatever it is, okay."

"When you creep a house, I want you to promise it will never be me or Chrissy."

Marc stared at the ground. "Don't you know it never could be? Never." His voice was trembling.

"I do now." I paused.

"So what's the second thing?" he asked gently.

Somehow saying it felt like I was telling my deepest secret. My voice was hushed.

"After you creep a house, I want you to tell me about it. Every detail."

"I told you that I knew you," Marc whispered. "From the first hour, I knew you." He said it with his eyes closed. Like a prayer.

Em called a couple of times and she e-mailed me constantly, but I now put her in the Them category. Em and I used to be the Us against Them, but now she was the voice of disapproval, the critic. When I told Marc about it, all about Em, he kind of hemmed and hawed.

"What?" I asked.

"Em called you 'Tweety Bird' and she kind of always ran the show, right?"

"Yes, but—"

"Sounds like she was always making herself the big authority. She went to shrinks so she knew how your mom was going to start acting about money. She was the one doling out the information about your father."

"Sure, but Earl was the one who—"

"So wasn't she always more or less controlling you,

and now that you're not doing what she wants you to do—she's acting like she's the cop and you're the criminal?" Marc shrugged. "I'm not sure she was ever much different than your parents."

I thought a minute and was still shopping for an answer when he delivered the final blow.

"It always bothered me," Marc said.

"What?"

"When Emily sent Chrissy that box of bears. Why didn't she send you anything? Just some little thing to make you feel better. She knew you had to be in the dumps. Why not a prepaid cell phone? She's got that kind of cash, right?"

Why hadn't she?

I even had a card from Robin waiting for me when I got to Brokedown Palace. But I had to go wagging after Em first.

I stopped answering Em's e-mail. If I couldn't avoid her calls, I didn't say much and ended them as quickly as I could. Marc and I were Us now, and everyone else was Them.

*   *   *

Two days later my cell rang, late. I was groggy when I answered.

"I did it. Last night," Marc said. His voice was harsh and breathy like when we had sex.

"Did what?"

"Creeped a house. With the gun. The sawed-off."

The dark thing raced up my neck. I rubbed my arms where the gooseflesh appeared. "Tell me."

"Big house. Rich neighborhood. He's a frickin' traffic court judge. They think they are so untouchable that the back door was unlocked and the security system was off. Being rich must make you stupid."

I thought back to the times we had gone to bed without checking the locks. We often left the security system unarmed because we had been the only ones to trip it.

"Just tell me," I said.

"I went in the back. It was like a changing room for the pool, then a hall. I cruised around and eyeballed their stuff. All kinds of crystal and stuff in special cabinets. They even had a library with shelves all the way to the ceiling. Why didn't they just wallpaper the place with money if they needed to impress people so bad?"

My mouth was dry. Em's house had a library like that. We used to play on the ladder that rolled along the floor.

"Did you watch them sleep?"

He groaned. "Ahh, you *so* should have been there. I've never had a rush like that. Full body flight then dive into ice water, stick your finger in the light socket, mix a handful of heavy drugs, bang the headboard sex total turn-on."

I was certain sex with me had never met those qualifications.

"I went in the girl's room first, but she was too ugly or something about her didn't give me any electricity. It's like she was practically dead anyway, so what was the point?"

Practically dead anyway. *Anyway?*

"I followed the old man's snores. Door was open and I strolled in, my sawed-off hanging down my side, just watching them sleep. The woman was toned-looking, and the guy was a *whale*. Full-scale orca. On his back, mouth open, sounding like he was cutting wood then gargling on the sawdust."

I could picture them.

"I got me a little souvenir, too," Marc bragged.

"You took something?"

"I got a traffic ticket a few months ago. Totally bogus. So I went to court. This judge wouldn't even listen. So I wanted something of his."

"Wait, you knew this guy?"

"Yeah, I just said. Judge that ruled on the ticket. Pay attention."

"Sorry, what did you take?"

"A gold key chain, shaped like a stop sign and says *STOP* on the front. On the back in fancy script it says *Go Get 'Em, Judge*. I found it still in its box pushed into the back of his desk drawer. I guess he didn't like it," Marc said.

"Marc, you'll get someone else in trouble."

"Who? Like I care?"

"They'll blame the housekeeper or her kids or their kids' friends," I said.

Silence. "You know you're bringing me down? Just shut up if you want to hear. If you want to be your mother, I got better people to talk to."

"No," I said before he could hang up on me. "Please, Marc, I want to hear. Forget what I said."

Marc didn't speak, but he didn't hang up. Finally— "This judge has it in for me. Just like the police do. If I go one mile over the limit, they ticket me. They know what happened in California."

"I thought your record was sealed in California?"

Again there was a long silence on the line.

"Sorry. Tell me more about the creeping."

"It was awesome. Thinking they don't know they are inches from death. I can blast them to hell and back and they won't even know. I have total power."

I thought when he told me all of this that my heart would still. That it would stop drumming for a moment. Instead it hammered, pounded, and thrummed. It sang mad music in Dorian mode. Slightly atonal. I closed my eyes and listened to my heart's new, strange melody.

I thought I fell in love with Marc. I did fall. Maybe it was a kind of love. But it had nothing to do with Marc. But fall...yeah, that's what I did.

PASSIVE IS THE LIE

Mom went nuts the next day. "Ames, get in here now!" First I rolled my eyes, then I rolled out of bed. She was pointing at her basket of clothes I'd left in her room. "Look at those."

"Why, are they doing tricks?"

The slap whipped my chin all the way to my collarbone.

"Do NOT try to be funny with me. I'm not in the mood to be disrespected."

"Couldn't happen," I said. Slow and cold, imitating

Marc in his cobra stage. "I'd have to respect you first."

This time I caught her left hand in the air before it landed on my face. I squeezed it hard, making her rings bite into her flesh.

"Don't touch me again," I said. I saw a hesitation and possibly a flicker of fear in Mom's eyes, but it was soon replaced with rage.

"You ruined all of my delicates!" she screeched. She grabbed a wad of her underthings, expensive silk, lace, wisps of finery, the pale tones grayed and the fabrics wrinkled and waddled like an old woman's skin.

"If it makes you feel any better, mine are like that, too. The woman at the Laundromat said that commercial washers and dryers aren't made for stuff like that."

"You aren't hand-washing them? You should have been washing all this by hand." Mom was still in screech mode.

I stared at her. "Wash your *underwear* by hand? Wash your own underwear, bitch."

I spun on a heel and was gone before she could grab me. I ran straight into Dad's body block.

"What did you call your mother?" he asked.

"Nothing you haven't," I dared him.

"Go to your room and stay there," he said.

Pretty day. Pretty family.

I slammed into my room and onto my bed, grabbed my phone. Chrissy was curled up, pressing the pillow against her ears.

"You don't have to answer to them anymore," Marc seethed after I told him what happened. "They were told not to touch you. They gave up all rights to you by laying a hand on you. Get that?"

I touched my cheek. I got that. I'd gone from someone they loved to someone they used to someone they hated. Yes, I got that.

"Don't fight with them. If you don't want to do something, don't. Act like you're listening and are agreeing to do what they say, then walk away and don't do it. Passive aggressive."

"I'm not big on passive," I said.

"Passive is the lie, aggressive is the truth," Marc said.

*   *   *

I woke up to scratching on my window screen. Marc. I opened the screen and climbed out. We went to his truck and then to his house. Marc unzipped his pants and resentment stirred in me. I had to perform like a circus seal before he would even talk to me? Didn't it matter to him that I didn't like the sex?

After, he rolled off me and rooted around in his nightstand. "Close your eyes and put out your hand."

Something cold and metallic coiled into my palm.

"Okay, you can look."

A key chain. Gold. A stop sign on the end.

"I want you to have it. It gives me a total buzz just to look at it. Makes me feel, like, *indestructible* knowing I stood over those people and held their lives in my hands. I want you to feel that kind of power. If you ever feel... confused or get scared or weak...get this out and hold it. We'll be connected."

I knew what it meant to him. It was practically like he was giving me an engagement ring.

"Marc...thank you."

"Goes without saying, no one else can see it. I could go to jail if anyone recognizes that thing."

"You can trust me," I said.

Marc sighed. "Listen, I've been thinking. We need to have a plan."

"A plan?"

"Sure. This can go on for a while. Maybe a long time, but sooner or later, we're going to get caught. I won't let your parents break us up."

"How could they do that? They already told us we can't see each other. That's working out really well for them." I kissed his flat stomach.

"They could send you away," he said. "If they checked and found out how old I am they could send me away. To prison."

I sat up. "What can we do?"

Marc put both hands behind his neck. "Let's not worry about that right now. It's complicated. There's no reason for your dad to suspect that I'm not seventeen, right?"

Em knows, I thought. *But she'd never tell Dad that*...
"No, you look like one of those guys the feds would put in a high school to work narc duty. Baby face."

"Careful, I've smashed a guy's teeth out with a piece of pipe for calling me that." He smoothed my hair back and kissed my forehead. "I do have a plan. If it gets bad and your parents come down on us—threaten us or something—we have to get serious and strike before they can. At the first sign of trouble, tell me. The first night possible you wait until they go to sleep, then call me on the cell. Unlock the back door. I come and take care of them, and then you, the munchkin, and me take off for parts unknown. Canada, maybe, or better, Mexico."

"Take care of them?" I asked.

Marc grabbed me by the shoulders and turned me to face him. "This isn't a game. When they get tired of batting you around, they'll start on your little sister."

I was stunned to silence. He dug his fingers into my flesh and shook me. "Are you strong enough to do something to stop it?"

I felt panic at his sudden fury, but his words about Chrissy shoved me over the edge. I clutched the key chain to my chest.

"If they try to separate me from you or me from Chrissy—they deserve anything they get."

ANYTHING THEY GET

The end came in two acts. Two nights. The first night the phone rang in the living room. Dad answered. I heard his voice, first in a hushed murmur, then getting louder.

My cell vibrated. "I'm parked on the street just out your window. Come play," Marc said.

It was a risk, knowing that Dad was awake, but I boosted out of the window and into the truck anyway. Marc had me out of my cutoffs by the time our first kiss was over. We were making love when I heard him.

"*Ames!*"

Marc and I looked up, scrambling, to see Dad framed in my bedroom window. He was screaming my name. Roaring like a wild, wounded beast.

"Ames!"

He lurched away from the window and appeared at the truck before I could struggle back into my clothes. Marc was back in the driver's seat, but I was still groping for clothes and it was easy for Dad to jerk me out of the truck.

I fell onto the asphalt pavement, and the loose gravel and rough surface cut and scraped my naked lower half.

"This isn't over. I know all about you. I know how old you are. I know about your record!" Dad shouted, jabbing one finger at Marc. "Get the hell out of here!" He slammed the truck door. Marc backed up then sped away, tires squealing.

I thought he was supposed to protect me...?

When we got into the house, Dad went ballistic.

"That kid isn't a kid. He's twenty-two years old."

I finally had my clothes on, but my blush was not about my nakedness.

"You knew!" he accused.

"So what?" I shouted back.

Mom wasn't shouting, though. Her words were so tentative I almost didn't recognize her voice. "Ames, you've been...intimate with this...man?" She sounded bewildered. And sad.

"This *man*," Dad spat, "has a sealed juvenile record, but he was out of juvie when he was eighteen, and when he was nineteen he went to trial for statutory rape of a fourteen-year-old girl. The father dropped the charges and refused to testify when they found their dog's body on their front porch. Their cocker spaniel had fifteen bullet holes in her."

He watched my reaction. "You didn't know that, did you?"

I wouldn't look at him.

"Marc's mother kicked him out because she was scared of him. She never wants him near her or her younger children again. His stepfather says he'll shoot him on sight."

"You're making all this up," I said. But I wasn't shouting. Wasn't I sure?

"Call Earl. Ask him yourself."

Em. Em had to have talked to Earl. Given him Marc's name and asked him to check him out. How many people would betray me?

Mom's voice was calm and...full of something I couldn't recognize. "Ames, go shower and wash those cuts carefully."

I opened my mouth to argue, but she shook her head and I saw tears in her eyes. "Ames, please. Go."

I was prepared for her anger. Dad's rage was easy to counter with my own. I might even understand Mom freezing me out, refusing to speak to or look at me, but I didn't understand this abrupt personality spin.

I showered and put some medicine on the cuts and scrapes I could reach. Mom came in. She took the tube and turned me around to attend to the cuts on the back of my thighs. "Ames, this is over with Marc. Your father is angry, but...I think I know what you were searching for. I'm sorry...that...you couldn't find it here."

Mom was saying she was sorry? Had she ever said she was sorry? What was going on?

She sighed. She was uncomfortable. Fiddling with the

ointment tube. Searching for words. She sat on the closed toilet and pulled up her legs until she rested her chin on her knees. "I looked for...security and called it love before, too." She slid her eyes toward the door. Toward Dad. "I thought for a long time that it was love." She shifted her attention back to me. "I didn't realize what you'd been going through. Not until tonight." She covered her mouth with one hand and closed her eyes. She looked like someone in pain. Then she stretched her legs back out and squeezed ointment onto her finger.

Her touch on my wounds was gentle. "There, I think that's all. The ones that I can see."

I turned to face her. "Mom..."

"No more discussion. Right now we're all too emotional. You are not leaving the house."

"Mom..."

"Ames, be prepared. Your father and I are going to file statutory rape charges on Marc."

"You can't. He didn't rape me. I wanted to."

"That's what we'll talk about later. When he's twenty-two and you're fifteen and confused..." Mom took my chin in her hand. "Marc is a predator. You don't understand that yet. Did you listen to what your father said? Did you hear about that girl's pet?" I jerked my face away.

"Your father wants to go to the police tonight, but he's practically incoherent, and I want to get a lawyer before we file charges."

Mom left the bathroom and I stood a minute, alone, mind spinning. Dog? Fifteen bullet holes? Why would Earl lie about something like that? But Marc was all I had. I rubbed my face with both hands. Was he? A few minutes ago Mom had been...who had she been?

Whoever, whatever. I didn't want Marc in prison because of me.

I called Marc.

"You have to get out of here," I whispered.

"What did he do?"

"My parents are going to put you in jail for statutory rape. They're going to talk to a lawyer tomorrow. You have to leave tonight."

"What do you mean *I* have to leave tonight? Are you

bailing on me? Nobody takes you away from me. It's just us, remember?"

A deep shiver passed over me. Just us? Wasn't Chrissy supposed to be part of this? I shook it off. I had to trust him. From the first hour, he knew me.

"I know," I said. "This is happening too fast. You need to get out of here and then—"

"No. It's plenty easy to take care of this right now."

I heard loud banging. I clicked off the phone and ran out to find Dad nailing boards across my window. Mom sighed. "I know those boards aren't going to keep you in your room. Your father is just venting." She nodded toward the front door. "I'm not going to lock you in, but if you leave this house tonight, you simply will not be allowed back. Not ever."

My mother and I stared each other down in silence.

"Ames, I sincerely believe you don't want to go that far."

"It has to be tonight," Marc said when I called back. "They've pushed us into a corner. I'll go to jail for years if they do this."

"But it's not rape, and..."

"Don't be naive. Your parents aren't rich now, but they know people. They know people who can make things happen. If your dad wants me in prison, that's where I'm going to be. And the rape that happens *there* won't be statutory."

I froze. I wouldn't just be abandoning Marc, I would be allowing my dad to destroy him.

How did I end up here?

"There's no choice, is there, Ames? Do you want those people to keep doing this to you? To control your life to make it hell every single day? They messed up their own lives and want you to pay the price? Want me to go to prison for it? Make you live like a slave, never get to go to school, have a boyfriend, do anything but wash their clothes and cook their food while your dad gambles and your mother bitches?"

I didn't say anything.

"You have the power to do something. Do something now. End this. Come with me. I'm the only one who truly loves you, who'll take care of you. From the moment I met you, haven't I always done that?"

"But we can't..." I said.

"It will be easy. Plenty easy."

"There's no way my dad is going to sleep tonight. It won't work."

Marc revised the plan a little. Tomorrow night, not tonight. We hung up, and I stared sleeplessly at the white ceiling. It held no clues, no answers.

Marc was my hero. But he did mean to kill my parents. I didn't have to do it. I didn't even have to watch. He would kill them and we would run to Mexico. We could be there by the morning after.

Why hadn't he mentioned Chrissy? He had made her a part of the plan, a part of "our family" when he talked about this before. Before it was real. Did that mean he would leave her in a house with dead bodies? Or would there be no witnesses?

I hated them.

Did they deserve to die?

They would put Marc in prison.

I would be alone in this hellhole...with them.

But…Mom had understood. Maybe we could start over.

Marc was going to kill my parents.

Maybe he wouldn't.

Yes. He would.

What was he going to do about Chrissy?

Could I let him do this?

Could I?

It was past two o'clock when I got up. I went to Mom and Dad's door and walked in.

"Mom, Dad." I stopped. I wasn't sure if I was going to sob or vomit.

"Ames, this is not the time—"

I rubbed my face with both hands, seeking composure. "Turn on a light. Please."

Mom switched on her bedside lamp.

I waited, knowing that everything was going to be different now, but not what path the different would take. I closed my eyes. *Just say it,* I told myself. I kept them closed while I spoke.

"Marc is planning to kill you, both of you. And I think maybe Chrissy."

I opened my eyes.

I thought Dad would yell or Mom would scream or cry, but we had all turned to salt. I don't think anyone breathed.

"Explain," Dad demanded. "All of it."

I inhaled deeply. Exhaled. "Please? You won't like what you hear. Can you not yell at me? Just listen until the end. This is hard."

Then Mom did cry. Tears rolled down her cheeks. "Oh, Ames," she whispered.

I clenched my fists. It poured out. I didn't get mad or shout. I told them like Chrissy would, like a reporter, listing the betrayals, the hurts, telling them finally how scared I had been and how they hadn't helped. How I had needed Marc, someone to make me feel safe. With his guns and his protectiveness. Now...I was in too deep. I didn't want what he was offering and I didn't know how to stop him.

"Ames," Mom said, "Do I hear you saying that you wanted Marc to kill us?"

I looked at her. I had to tell the truth. To make them understand how much danger they were in. "Yes," I said.

From the look on her face I may as well have shot her right then. I guess I got what I wanted. I had destroyed the Commander. It didn't feel good.

Dad said nothing. He looked at Mom. "We have to get out of here. Right now. I know how desperate young men can be. I know."

I closed my eyes and all my tensed muscles sagged. He believed me.

"You think he'd come in this house and kill us even if Ames tells him not to?" Mom said.

Dad looked at me. "I think if Ames tells him that—"

"He'll kill us all," I finished. "Because I abandoned him." Then I told them about creeping the judge's house. "My gut tells me that was practice. He wants to kill."

Mom covered her mouth. "You're right; we have to get out of here now. Tonight. Start packing the essentials." She turned to Dad. "Back to Boulder?"

But we hadn't counted on something. Someone.

Chrissy.

We went to wake her up. "Up and away, kiddo. We're going to Boulder," Dad said.

"I'm still sleeping," Chrissy said.

"I know, but we're in a hurry and you can sleep in the car," Mom said.

Chrissy sat up. "Why are all of you in my room? It's nighttime!"

"I'm telling her the truth," I told Mom. "Not telling the truth is how we got in trouble in the first place."

"She's too young," Mom resisted. "You'll scare her."

I turned to Chrissy. "Chrissy, you know how Marc gets mad?"

She nodded.

"He's real mad right now. At me and at Dad and Mom. He says he's going to hurt us because he's mad. I believe him."

"I believe him, too. He's mean when he's mad," Chrissy said.

"Yes, he is, and he is doing some really bad things. He's done them before. So we're going to go to Boulder. We're going to go tonight so he can't do bad things to us. We're going to pack fast and leave."

Mom and Dad turned to go.

"Wait." Chrissy startled us. "If Marc is bad and doing bad things, shouldn't he go to jail?"

Dad, Mom, and I looked at one another as if...well, why hadn't it occurred to us to call the police? All three of us were still lashing our rudders tight and sailing away in a straight line, running from any problem that came up. For months, we'd been running away from each other. Only Chrissy stood her ground and looked for the right answer.

SOME PEOPLE COUNT
MORE THAN OTHERS

A man came out of his office, introduced himself as a detective, and sat us down in uncomfortable chairs. He looked tired and didn't waste time. "Something about a death threat?" Dad gave him the synopsis rather than the novel.

"Are you sure we don't have a young girl with a case of buyer's remorse and wanting to get some revenge?"

I flushed but remained silent.

I saw Dad grappling with his anger. "I think if you check to see if Marc DeVayne got a traffic ticket in…"

"He said a few months ago," I said.

"Marc DeVayne, you say? We *have* had some dealings with Marc." The detective seemed much more interested now. He turned to me. "You saw guns in his house? You can testify to that?"

I nodded.

He leaned back in his chair. "Your boyfriend is not as clear of the law as he told you. He did a little B and E here in Texas. He's on parole, and if he's got guns, that breaks the terms... He can serve out his eighteen months in Huntsville."

"Eighteen months?" My mother leaned into the detective. "Don't you get it? He'll know my daughter turned him in. He'll make it his mission to find her and he'll kill all of us. Eighteen months means he'll be out in six. Just enough time to get his plans made and his fury stoked."

"Now you're going all conspiracy theory here. He's a bad guy, sure, but I don't think he would wait and plan and stalk..."

"He did with that judge," I said.

Silence.

The detective leaned forward this time. "Say again?"

"The house he creeped. It was the judge who gave him a traffic ticket. It made him mad."

"You should never make him mad. It's scary," Chrissy said.

"He found out where the judge lived and that's who he stood over with the shotgun. I can prove it." I reached into the pocket of my hoodie and pulled out the key chain. "Marc gave it to me after he stole it from the judge's house."

The detective took the chain with the tip of his pen and slid it into an evidence bag. He put up his hands like he was halting traffic and picked up the phone. "Pete, sorry to call so late. Yep, it's important. You own a key chain, gold fob, octagon shape, stop sign on the front, and—yep, that's what it says. I know because I'm holding it."

He looked at me. "Marc say where he got it?"

I nodded. "He said it was still in the box at the back of a drawer in the library."

"You hear all that, Pete?" Pause. "Yep, not only does that mean you were robbed, if everything I'm hearing is true, but somebody was in your bedroom, standing over you with a shotgun that night. Well, I don't know about attempted murder, maybe so, but the lawyers can sure make something out of it."

He hung up the phone. "We got ourselves one pissed-off judge."

The detective spread his hands fingers out on the desk. "This is what I think. I can't do much for you except bust DeVayne for parole violation. Now, his robbing a judge and maybe threatening his life"—he looked at Dad and shrugged—"that part will be tough to prove. Defense will say your daughter took the key chain and the threat is...he said, she said."

He cricked his neck. "But messing with a judge puts good old Marc right in the target sights of the Texas Rangers. Let me see what I can do going that route. Put this bad boy away for a long time."

"I don't care how you do it. As long as he doesn't come in my house with a gun," Dad said.

The detective looked out his window. "Sun's coming up. You folks think you'll be okay during the day?"

I nodded. Marc was friends with the dark.

THE DARK SONG

The house was dark and quiet. When I opened my bedroom door and listened, the breathing from my parents' room was steady and deep. The lump that was supposed to be Chrissy remained unmoving, face turned toward the wall, one arm circling her favorite bear.

It was time. The dark song welled up in me. I heard it just as Marc described it. Predator's heart singing to the heart of the prey. Saliva flooded my mouth, usually a precursor to the gag reflex. I swallowed hard and breathed deep, mouth open. Breathed out through my nose. Swallowed again. I punched the cell phone.

"Ames?" he asked without preamble. "You ready for this?"

I tiptoed away from my room into the living room and through to the kitchen.

"Are you sure they're asleep?" Marc asked. His voice was urgent but pumping with adrenaline.

"Do you have to do this, Marc? Finish it? Can't you take Chrissy and me away and make our own family?"

His voice was a caress but his words were a punch. "Ames, if we leave them alive, we'll never get away. There won't be time. They'll have border patrol to stop us hours before we get there. It's the only way. It will be just us when it's done. No one will ever hurt you again."

He didn't mention Chrissy. This was hard. Too hard. I was trapped now.

"Okay."

"Stomp on the phone, throw it around the place, but make sure the battery's in a different yard than the other pieces. Then go get in your bed. I'll do all the rest."

"The kitchen door is open," I said. "Let's get it done."

"Ames," Marc whispered. "I love you."

I punched the phone off, opened the back and removed one piece, pushing it deep into the pocket of my jeans, and then dropped the phone on the grungy linoleum floor. Two hard whacks with my heel set pieces of it skittering across the room. I separated the battery, stomped on it a few more times for good measure. I hurried to the backyard and side-armed the pieces into the heaps of trash and junk piles in the surrounding yards.

I stood for just a second on the porch, my hand on the knob of the kitchen door. Could I do this? My heart pounded and my mouth was so dry I couldn't swallow. Had I stepped so far over the line that I was capable of a betrayal this big? This horrible?

I opened the door.

Upstairs, I checked on the Chrissy lump and the one that represented me, then slid into my parents' room. I backed into a corner, deep into the shadows and waited. If this was going to happen, I needed to watch. I needed to see it all.

I didn't wait long. I heard the door squeak on the

hinge. I don't know if I heard Marc's breath or mine. I know I heard my heart pounding, pounding in my head. His sneakers made a muffled sound, like a mouse being strangled as he swept through the living room then slowed as he entered my parents' room.

I stilled my breath. Would he hear my heart?

Marc crept up to the side of the bed. My father's side. The sawed-off shotgun hung down along his left leg. From the trickle of moonlight I saw Marc close his eyes and inhale, deep and long. He jacked the shotgun one-handed, his muscles tensing then releasing. Pumping the shells, readying them for their work. He called the sound his shotgun serenade.

He raised the gun.

And...

The muzzle of a handgun pressed against the base of Marc's neck. "Drop it. Now."

The two sleeping figures that were not my parents sat up, handguns pointed at Marc's head and torso. The male officer said, "Put it down easy, boy. Do it."

The female officer was amped and her voice trembled a little. "Hold on to it a second longer and you give me an excuse, understand?"

I glided out of the shadows just as another officer flipped on the overhead light. Marc placed the shotgun on the nightstand. I watched his hands cuffed behind his back.

He stared at me, and I never looked away. Not even as I handed the phone's computer chip to another officer. Tears rolled down my cheeks. I was more than sure Marc misunderstood those tears.

"You." His voice was flat. Emotionless. "Who are you?"

He had asked the right question.

I didn't have an answer.

Who was I?

Who had I been?

Who would I be?

I don't know.

I do know this.

I am not innocent.

READER DISCUSSION QUESTIONS
DARK SONG

1. What does the title *Dark Song* mean to you? In what ways does it describe the events and relationships portrayed in the novel? Do you think what Marc tells Ames— that the song of darkness was always inside her—is true? Do you think everyone has a "darkness" inside them? Check out the interview with the author, Gail Giles, to see what she has to say about this topic.

2. As the novel opens, Ames says, "Christmas was near, and Boulder looked like a fairy tale. . . . Our house was a

fairy tale, too. . . . My mom wouldn't have it any other way." What can you infer about Ames's mother from this statement? How does Ames's mother's upbringing affect her needs for perfection and keeping up appearances? Ames seems to like her family's "perfection" at the beginning of the story, but how does her perception change after her family's financial downfall?

3. The author has said that one of her favorite characters in *Dark Song* is Earl, Em's father. Who do you think are the most interesting secondary characters in this story? What roles do you think Earl, Chrissy, and Em play? How would Ames's story have been different without her interactions with these characters? Do you think they do enough to assist Ames as she begins to spiral out of control?

4. In the first half of the story, Em tells Ames, "I've been trying to get this through your head since we were, like, ten. Parents lie. It's what they do." Do you agree with this? Are there times when a parent's choice to be dishonest with their children is the right thing to do? Can you think of a

time in your own life when one of your parents was untruthful but you understood their reasons for being so?

5. How would you describe Ames's and Marc's relationship? Would you use different words to describe it as the story progresses? Do you think that Marc really loves Ames, and if so, in what way?

6. In *Dark Song*, fear both motivates and incapacitates Ames. Do you think she deals with her fears well? Does she acknowledge that she's afraid? Is she able to turn to others for help? What are the consequences of her reactions?

7. Ames's mother, Diana, has a strained relationship with her own mother, Robin. What effect, if any, does that have on how Ames's and her mother's relationship falls apart? How is Ames's relationship with her mother similar to and different from Ames's relationship with her father?

8. Would you want to be friends with someone like Ames? What strengths does she have that might draw you to her?

Which of her weaknesses might push you away? Do you share any of these characteristics with Ames?

9. In the last line of the novel, Ames says, "I am not innocent." Why do you think the author chose to end the story this way, and do you think it is a satisfying ending? What do you think will happen to Ames and her family now?

10. Consider the novel's cover. How are the images symbolic of the events that take place throughout the story?

AN INTERVIEW WITH
GAIL GILES

1. Your inspiration for *Dark Song* came from your own research about several disturbing cases of violence involving young girls in relationships with older men. Can you explain your research in more detail and how you turned that research into Ames's story?

I watched a TV show about a young girl who developed a relationship with an older man, and her parents intervened. The girl was furious, and she and the boyfriend conspired for the boyfriend and a friend of his to kill her parents. This reminded me of the killing spree of Richard Starkweather and his young girlfriend, which began with the murder of her parents. Same scenario: young girl, older boyfriend, parental refusal that girl could see boy again. I decided to start researching whether this had happened any other times recently and was dismayed to find twenty-two cases of either one or both parents murdered as a result of parental interference in a young girl/older boyfriend situation. The cases ranged from Japan to Alaska. But the most shocking part was that I only had to search back eighteen months to find those twenty-two cases. It occurred to me that this phenomenon might be a sort of female version of Columbine. It seems as though boys tend to take their frustrations and anger out and away, and girls seem to pull their anger in and release it close to home.

2. As in your previous book, *Right Behind You*, the setting of *Dark Song* plays a large role in the story's plot. Can you describe what may have led you to set the two

halves of Dark Song in the very different locations of Colorado and Texas?

Colorado was one of the places where a murder of this type had occurred. Also, a cousin I love dearly lives in Boulder, Colorado, and this is kind of a hello to her.

As for Texas, it's where I was born and have lived the greater portion of my life. As a setting, it's a comfort zone for me.

3. In *Dark Song*, you created a character with a seemingly normal, happy life before everything she knows suddenly spirals out of control. Was the fragility of one's own circumstances a theme you consciously wove into the story? Did the economic recession and financial market meltdown of 2008 play into the plotline of Ames's father losing his job after nefarious investing?

I was writing the book in 2008, and the recession seemed to fit with the outward changes I needed for Ames's life. The recession couldn't just "happen" to the characters, though. The characters have to make the action happen, so I created the father's gambling and theft problems. The recession ended up being a nice by-product. However, the fragility of life's circumstances is certainly a theme I had in mind while writing, and how we all either pull together or pull apart was the central theme of the book. Ames summarizes this theme when she thinks to herself, "Did we just love each other when it was easy?"

4. Ames describes a "darkness" inside of her that grows throughout the story, and a number of your books feature characters whose "dark sides" win in the end. Do you believe that everyone has a kind of dark side, as well as the ability to overcome it, as Ames eventually does?

Certainly. I don't think we can have light without dark, good without bad, et cetera. Making the choice is what life is about and why I write books.

5. Marc's obsession with a fantasy of "creeping houses" is one of the scariest things I have ever read in

suspense fiction. You came up with the term "creeping houses," but where did you get the idea?

From a real case about two boys who killed a couple in Vermont. Before experiencing the thrill of killing, they wanted to experience the thrill of going through a stranger's house and touching all their things without the person ever knowing they had been there. The boys did this while the couple was away, and they also did it to someone else they knew. I decided to take it a step further and in a different direction, but the basic idea is the same.

6. You once said that Earl, who is only onstage for brief moments of the story, yet is ultimately essential to the plot, is your favorite character. Why is that? Do you have general thoughts about the supporting-role characters in your novels and how you approach them from a writing standpoint?

When you write dark novels, you can get lost in that dark. When you write unsympathetic characters, you can lose sight of what is good or right or moral. You have to have a touchstone character who keeps the center solid—to make it hold. That's Earl. He is good, moral, and likable. He knows who he is and is willing to help, but he also knows when someone is going wrong and needs guidance rather than judgment. I think he will agree that Ames is not innocent and help her find her way again.

I take supporting characters very seriously when I'm writing because they exist to do exactly as their name suggests: support the story. They must be invaluable to a story or they shouldn't be there at all. You never want an unnecessary character taking up space in your novel. I spend lots of time deciding who the touchstone character will be, why it will be who it is, and how that character will enter the picture and become that touchstone.

7. Was *Dark Song* an especially challenging book for you to write, and if so, why? Alternately, was there a part of creating this book that was particularly satisfying?

Dark Song was very challenging for me. It was incredibly hard to make Ames a sympathetic character in any way, because like the girls in the real cases I researched, she spirals out of control very quickly and seems to forget about anyone but herself in the process. It took so many revisions and help from my editor, Andrea Spooner, and her assistant, Jill Dembowski, to lead me in the proper direction.

Alternately, I loved writing Marc. I know—he's despicable, the baddest of the bad boys—but there was something wounded and vulnerable in him. I wanted to show how Ames could become attracted to him and fall so hard for him.

8. Your books are known for having characters with authentic teenage viewpoints. How do you write so convincingly from a teen perspective?

I remember vividly. Seriously, that's about it. I can still get that pain that tends to fade from our memories as we grow older. Many adults call it angst, but I still feel it as pain, and I channel that as I'm writing my books about these terribly painful and complex situations.

9. Your books are also known for tackling controversial topics, especially teen violence, and this leads to different interpretations of and reactions to your work. What do you hope readers will take away from your books, specifically *Dark Song*?

Everyone has a dark side. Experience it through reading, not life. Stay on the right side of the cell bars. That is why I want to make my books a visceral read, so nobody has to experience that darkness again in life.

I know it's uncomfortable to read about some of my characters. I have received negative responses to my writing from readers who think I support or condone the actions of my characters. I don't. But I accept that this behavior exists, and I think we have to understand it to change it. Merely judging behavior doesn't change it. Even self-judgment doesn't help if you don't understand the root cause. Exposing things to open air is often not pleasant, but I think it's necessary for healing.

Some of my readers come to my books to be healed. Others come to learn to understand others. Some come to be entertained. I want to reach as many as I can.

10. What kind of writing routine do you have? Is there a specific time and order in which you do things, or do you just allow inspiration to come as it will?

I have a two-step routine that I follow. The first part is that I must write daily, and I have to write at least three hundred words a day or sit there for three hours, whichever comes first. I'd much rather get the three hundred words in. The second part is that I end the day's writing in the middle of a sentence, in the middle of a paragraph, in the middle of a page, in the middle of a chapter. That way the next day, I'm sure I can finish the sentence, and I'm pretty sure I can finish the paragraph, and by that time I'm feeling like I can finish the page, and now I'm rolling to finish the chapter. But then I know I can't quit at the end of a chapter, so. . . . Inspiration follows on the heels of work ethic. If you wait for the muse—well, the muse is lazy, and so am I.

Gail Giles is the acclaimed author of several psychological drama/suspense novels for teens, including *What Happened to Cass McBride?*, *Shattering Glass*, and *Right Behind You*, all of which received numerous starred reviews and awards. She lives in The Woodlands, Texas, with her husband and three dogs. Her website is www.gailgiles.com and her blog is notjazz.livejournal.com.